Someone Like You

By J.R. Zimmer

Book three
Fisher/Lafayette Saga

Badlanders Press

Someone Like You

©2020 by Janette Walker

All rights reserved

Edited by Julie Baltzell

Cover design by Janette Walker

Model Image Credit:(c) photosvit www.fotosearch.com

ISBN 9781737626909

Cover design by Janette Walker

This book is the copyrighted property of the author and may not be reproduced, scanned, or distributed for any commercial or non-commercial use and may not be resold or given away. No alteration of content is allowed.

Your support and respect for the property of this author is appreciated. Thank you!

This is a work of fiction. Names, characters and incidents are products of the author's imagination or are used fictitiously and are not to be construed as real, or historically accurate.

Fisher/Lafayette Saga

If There Hadn't Been You

Now and Forever

Someone Like You

Spitfire

Something Magical

Coming Home (Free Ebook when signing up for my newsletter at www.jrzimmer.com. Not available anywhere else.)

The Dreamer

Eagle's Wolf

For

My Aunt & Uncle:

Judy & Duane Miller

(Duane passed away too young.
He will always be in our hearts.)

Thank you for having an epic “how we met” story.

Someone Like You

by J.R. Zimmer

Chapter One

February 1976

Most days, Cadman Benson was in a good mood.

Today was not one of them.

As he climbed into his 1975 Black Pontiac Firebird, he considered telling the President of the United States to take the job and shove it up his ass. It would not have been the first time he had had the same thought in his eleven-year career.

Had the task force not recently completed a successful hostage-rescue mission in Iraq?

Yes, they had.

Did the American people know this had happened?

No, they did not. Why? Because according to the government, the team did not exist. It was part of a confidential organization that only a few select officials knew about. The fewer people involved, the easier the secret was to keep, which was key to the team's success and of course, deny ability.

But it sure would be nice if the president would thank the team occasionally instead of reprimanding him when things went wrong. Like the incident involving the helicopter and the power lines in Eilat. They had no choice but to engage the kidnappers when they tried to fight back.

Sure, the team lost a helicopter, but more importantly, the team was successfully able to extract all the hostages, including that goddamn Senator, who now claimed he suffered trauma during the extraction and was demanding someone pay.

Pay for what? Saving his dumbass?

Stupid shit.

The man shouldn't have been in Iraq in the first place, knowing it was never stable enough for anyone to be there.

Cadman started the engine as he contemplated kidnapping the Senator in question and delivering him back into the hands of the ones who had abducted him in the first place. Perhaps the man would rather be "traumatized" by them.

Those people wouldn't handle the pussy with gentle hands.

Shit head.

Placing the car in reverse, Cadman jettisoned out from the parking space. Knowing he should have looked first, before hearing, "Fucking A! Watch where you're going!" being screamed at him.

Cadman did not care. He didn't bother to stop the vehicle or apologize. He slammed the gear shift into drive and shot forward out of the White House parking lot.

"Your team should have been more careful," President Ford said. "The Senator wants heads to roll."

Whatever.

Ford could soothe the Senator's ruffled feathers, and this would all wash under the bridge, but damn it, men had risked their lives for that whinny son-of-a-bitch!

Perhaps the fact this was an election year had something to do with Cadman's added frustration. Not knowing who would be elected and then ultimately become the new leader of Task Force Ghost always put him in a foul mood.

Ford was the third president to have the responsibility to give directives to the task force since it first formed in 1965 under Lyndon B. Johnson.

Johnson had put this group of elite commandos together after Congress passed the Gulf of Tonkin Resolution in 1964. It granted Johnson the power to use military force in Southeast Asia without having to ask for an official declaration of war.

Officially Cadman handpicked the members. President Johnson hand-picked him to lead the best of the best men that would be-come Task Force Ghost.

Cadman had been a Secret Service agent for eight years before Johnson offered him the position to head up the special op. Before that, he had been a twelve-year Marine. With thirty-one years of service to the United States under his belt, he was not worried about a Senator who had been 'traumatized.'

But it pissed him off to have the president bitch about it instead of thanking the team for getting all the hostages back safe and sound.

Cadman pointed his car in the direction of the mall, intending to pick up a new down-filled vest. There was a sale on today at one of the department stores, and he needed a new one since his one-year-old German shepherd had taken it upon himself to use his last one as a chew toy. Besides, maybe taking some time to look through the clearance racks would help him put this whole thing from his mind and calm him down.

Perhaps Ford would lose the election, and the next president would be more appreciative of the men's efforts.

Thinking about who the potential candidates were would only give him indigestion if he were to dwell on it. He figured Ford would probably get the Republican endorsement; however, if that happened, Cadman would not be happy with the choice. Perhaps it was wrong to hope your current boss would be out of a job, but Cadman had never been a fan of Ford.

However, out of respect for the office of the Presidency, Cadman largely avoided questioning the orders from the person holding the

position. Besides, if Ford was re-elected, there was much to be said for the expression: better the devil you know than the one you don't. A new President always meant an unsettling adjustment period for the White House staff and those under the president's command.

As far as Cadman was concerned, the democrats running for their party's nomination weren't much better than Ford.

As the mall came into view, Cadman pushed thoughts of the election from his mind; there was no point thinking about something he couldn't control.

He found a parking space opening that was close to the main entrance of the shopping center. At least something was going right for him today.

With any luck, he'd find a vest in no time and be on his way home…

As he was exiting his car, he suddenly remembered the promise he'd made his mother three months ago: to stop by her house today and put up the shelves in her bedroom. "Damn it!" he thought. Why couldn't he have remembered that before leaving the house this morning so he could have grabbed the tools he needed on his way out?

Knowing his mother would likely disown him if he canceled yet again, he resolved to stop at the hardware store on the way to her place and buy the necessary items. He was in no mood to drive across town to his own place for tools, only to backtrack to her house. At least this way, he could leave the new set at his mother's, just in case some unexpected "Honeyboy" projects popped up down the road.

With a resigned sigh, he walked into the mall, hoping to find a down vest on sale that fit his 6 foot, two-hundred-pound frame. It didn't really have to be a bargain price. He had funds. The government paid him well, but he enjoyed finding good deals.

As he was looking through the racks of vests, pulling one out to try on, he heard a voice from behind him say, "Good god, Benson. I thought

for sure you never ventured beyond your office or otherworldly activities."

Cadman turned and grinned at the man standing on the other side of the clothing rack.

Gary Davidson was one member of the force, a local operative who worked as a mechanic at the Last Stop Garage when not needed for a mission. All the men in the unit, except Cadman, maintained civilian jobs to keep a low profile and blend with the public. Cadman strategically had his operatives spread across several states rather than clustered together. When he wasn't organizing a mission, Cadman spent his weekdays in an office building near the White House. His job was to monitor the world's illegal activities and prepare his specialized team to step in when the regular military could not handle the situation.

Taking the vest, he'd tried on off, he grabbed another one from the rack and slipping it on, as he told Gary, "I get out of my hole once in a while. Sometimes I frequent a grocery store too."

Laughing, Gary put a hand over his heart and said, "Be still my heart! You mean, you eat?"

They bantered back and forth until Cadman located the vest he wanted. "Nice chatting with you," he said to Gary, quickly adding, "I have an appointment." He saw no reason to elaborate that the appointment was only his mother waiting for help.

"Sure," Gary said, understanding Cadman's excuse to leave, but he still fell into step with him as Cadman made his way toward the checkout counter. "By the way," Gary added casually, "what did your boss say about that job we did for him?"

Cadman stopped, turned toward him, and refused to make this guy's day into a downer.

"He was happy as a clam."

Gary grinned ear-to-ear. “That’s great! What did he say about the bird?”

“That part he wasn’t pleased about, but those things happen.”

No point mentioning that Ford was considering having the Ghost Team pay for its replacement out of their paychecks over the next ten years. Finding money to replace equipment destroyed by a team that didn't officially exist was nearly impossible. The Ghost Team was not listed in any government budget under anything relating to the military. Instead, those in charge hid the necessary funding in legislative bills marked for entirely different causes—a classic trick. The government loved stashing budgets inside bills that Congress would pass without batting an eye, knowing full well no one ever read them thoroughly.

The two men started walking again. Reaching the checkout area, Gary paused to snatch a magazine, then nudged Cadman. "See that?" he said, tapping the cover image. "She could definitely make a guy forget his troubles!"

Half-expecting Gary to be pointing at Farrah Fawcett, the actress who had men across the United States lusting over her in the new television series Charlie’s Angels, Cadman was shocked to see he was wrong. He was even more surprised when Rosalinda Lafayette's cat-like green eyes stared out at him from the cover of the magazine. The headline read: "Rosalinda! French Actress Expecting Second Child, Eleven Years After Giving Birth to Her Son."

Gary paged through the magazine until he found the story. “Can you believe it? Wow. I can’t believe she would wait that long to have another baby.”

Cadman wanted to shut down the conversation about Rosalinda immediately. He knew the heartache she and her husband had endured over the years, desperately wanting a house full of children, only to face the reality that Rosalinda might never have more than one. Cadman knew the Lafayettes personally; in fact, he was an honorary uncle to the boy,

loving eleven-year-old Mason as though he were his own son. Regardless of the circumstances of Mason's conception, the child never lacked love. Cadman's mind flashed back almost nine months: he had been visiting the Lafayettes in Paris when Rosalinda burst into her husband's office, tears in her eyes, and announced she was pregnant.

It was an announcement that all of France wanted to celebrate. The country loved Rosalinda and her husband, Charles.

Cadman was determined not to reveal his connection to the couple. That was his private life, and he would guard it fiercely. He dismissed Gary's curiosity with a terse comment: "Gary, you're acting like a gossipy old woman."

With a hoot of laughter, Gary put the magazine back on the rack, much to Cadman's relief, and said, "Boss, admit it. She's gorgeous."

To himself, Cadman said, absolutely, but for Gary, he only shrugged. He wanted to be done with this conversation.

"No wonder you're not married," Gary grumbled under his breath.

Cadman chuckled. "I like women, but I don't need one in my life."

"Spoken like a die-hard bachelor."

Laughing, Cadman paid for the vest, said goodbye to Gary, and headed for his car.

The next stop was the hardware store, then his mothers.

He glanced at his watch. The teenager he hired to walk the dog a few times a day would have last been at the house about an hour ago. That would give Cadman a few hours to get those shelves up before the dog would need to be let out once more.

Why he had got a dog in the first place, Cadman wasn't sure. Perhaps for the companionship it offered. It was nice to come home and have the big lug greet him at the door. Thankfully, he had found a dog sitting service he could depend upon to take care of Mutt on short notice or

when he had to leave on a mission that had him not knowing how long he would be gone.

Before leaving the mall, Cadman put the new vest on.

Not that the day was overly cold, but the wind had picked up, and thirty-seven degrees above zero would feel a lot more comfortable with the added protection.

Someone Like You

Chapter Two

Cadman had been in this hardware store a few times over the years since moving back to Washington, D.C., ten and a half years ago from New York. Being in D.C. made meetings with the president and upper brass a lot easier than having phone conversations. Besides, he grew up in the area, and it was nice to have family close by.

This hardware store went by the name Nuts, Bolts, and a Whole Lot More. It was a friendly enough establishment and sold a wide variety of items. Paint, tools, lawn and garden supplies, and other odds and ends one might not have thought they needed until they saw it strategically placed on the shelf.

Finding all the items he intended to purchase, he began making his way to the cash register. Of course, there was a line. This could not be the quick in-and-out deal he had hoped for. With a sigh, he moved to the back of the line, his eyes roaming easily over the heads of the other customers waiting their turn, a benefit of being six feet tall.

He counted heads.

Ten. Ten people ahead of him.

It sure would be nice if the cashier ringing up this horde of people would notice she had a clear line to Cincinnati and call someone for assistance.

Glancing at the cashier, to see if she noticed the lane jam, made him think perhaps having to stand here longer than he initially would have liked would not be half bad. The woman at the counter was easy on the eyes.

Cadman liked the shoulder-length frosted blond hair that fell forward as she looked down at an item to bag it, and he really liked the way she

flipped that gorgeous mane back out of the way each time it strayed forward. She appeared to be somewhere between thirty-five to forty years old, and if she had any gray hair, the highlights of her curls hid it.

He had his own gray hair infiltrating his head of hair, and the short beard he grew out seven years ago. The gray came with age, and with age came the knowledge that he could not continue joining his team much longer on the missions they undertook. The task force needed people with speed and flexibility, and Cadman was not vain enough to pretend he was not slowing down a tad. It might be time to send the team out on their own while he managed the operation from his office.

Ugg. He knew it was something he would have to get used to. Even though he would miss the adventure, he refused to cripple his team by not admitting his own mortality.

Now there were only five people ahead of him. It surprised him how quickly the line dwindled down. The woman was obviously efficient at her job and did not waste steps.

Great, smile, ring items, bag, and collect the money. Her movements seemed like a well-rehearsed dance.

Finally, when it was his turn at the counter, she turned and flashed him a brilliant smile that actually made his heart skip a beat. That felt ridiculous to him. He was not the type of man who swooned over women; he might find them attractive and flirt, but that was it. Still, he decided, he wouldn't complain if this particular woman occupied his dreams tonight.

Cadman lived his life as a confirmed bachelor and liked the idea of never being tied down. Well, not in the commitment sense. He was not immune to a beautiful woman, and this one was just that. Beautiful.

There were a few women over the years he fantasized about, including Rosalinda Lafayette, who had been his lover before she married her husband. Those encounters were always memorable to him, but it had been nothing more than sex. It was great, passionate sex they enjoyed;

probably better because there were no strings or commitment. They both knew their connection was limited to what they shared between the sheets from time to time. The trysts ended before she married her husband, though they remained good friends, but that fact did not put an end to the memories. Even after all these years of shared passion and the starlet's ability to make him her willing "boy toy," those memories still invaded his dreams.

"Hi," the cashier said, and her killer smile had thoughts of Rosalinda fleeing from his mind. "Did you find everything you needed?"

Guys loved openings like that. So many answers came to mind. Sentences like, "Yeah, now that I found you, I'm complete." Or "I thought I did until I saw you."

Cadman refused to be one of those guys, so instead, he said, "I believe I have. Thanks."

Seriously, could he have said anything more unimpressive?

"That's great." She turned that smile on him again. He almost wished she would stop doing that. Every time she beamed that brilliant smile at him, his thought process seemed to slow down.

Like now. When she announced the total of his purchases. Apparently, he had not heard her correctly. It sounded as though she said, "One hundred fifty-nine dollars and forty-nine cents."

Cadman blinked, glancing down at her name badge, he shook his head. "I'm sorry, Kasey. I didn't hear you correctly. What's my total?"

She repeated it. With a straight face, as though this was not a joke. "One hundred fifty-nine dollars and fifty-nine cents."

"For a screwdriver, a box of screws and a level?!" His voice almost boomed. He was indignant. He knew the country was suffering from inflation, but this was beyond absurd.

"Well, no," she amended, looking almost shy and hesitant. "The screwdriver, screws and level aren't very expensive..."

Ha! Damn right they weren't!

"But," she lowered her voice, leaned toward him, and whispered, "you forgot about the vest."

He stared at her. "Excuse me?"

With a subtle movement of her chin, she told him, "That vest you're wearing adds the hundred dollars to the bill."

Speechless. That's what he was. She was accusing him… him of all people, of shoplifting!

"Lady! I just purchased this vest at the mall! It's mine!"

The stupid blond had the nerve to smirk.

He could not believe he'd thought she was pretty. Ha! That little sneer of hers took her looks down a few notches in Cadman's mind.

"I have the goddamn receipt!" He jammed his hands into the pockets of the vest, searching for the proof of his claim. It was when he could not find the receipt he remembered throwing it in the glove compartment of his Firebird, to add to the other receipts he always tossed there to file later.

"It's in my car."

She nodded as though she'd expected that. "Sure, it is."

He sputtered. "Now listen here! I'll just go out to my car and get the receipt."

"Not with that vest on, you won't."

By now, others in the store were gathering, taking in the drama.

Cadman could feel his face beginning to flush red. "I want to speak to your manager."

With a tight smile, she said, "Certainly. One moment." She turned around; turned back. "Hi, what can I help you with?"

He began to vibrate. “You’re the manager?”

She pointed to her name badge.

There it was, plain as day. Kasey E. - Manager. He missed that the first go-round when he thought she was pretty.

His flush went to the roots of his hair.

He was livid, to say the least.

“You don’t even sell vests….”

She pointed to a rack of them behind him.

Without a word, he removed his vest with quick angry movements, handed it to her. “That better still be here when I come back with my goddamn receipt!”

“Sure,” she said in a voice, sounding as though she did not believe he would be back at all.

The desire to strangle her was strong.

Annoyed, Cadman marched out the door at a quick strut, but slow enough to hear her say calm as you please, “I can help the next person in line.”

He absolutely could not believe this was happening to him!

Swearing a blue streak all the way to his car, he retrieved the proof of purchase and marched back into the store. Not caring he was interrupting the transaction of an innocent bystander, Cadman threw the ticket on the counter and told her, “Give me my vest.”

The woman took the paper; glanced down at it. To Cadman’s satisfaction, her face turned a bit red upon seeing the proof of purchase. But she did not offer an apology as she handed him back his vest.

“Can I have my other items too?” Cadman asked with scorn.

“Certainly. As soon as you pay for them.”

Cadman glanced at his watch. If it was not for the fact he was now behind schedule, he would have walked out and gone to another store.

Manager Kasey finished the transaction she'd been in the middle of when Cadman interrupted, thanked the man, then turned to Cadman. Without a word to him, she rang up the items. She told him the total, took his money, bagged the items, and had the gall to say, "Have a wonderful day."

He wanted to hit something.

The fact he heard others in the store break out into laughter was the icing on the cake.

His job was to protect the people of the United States from terrorists, but that was one dimwit he would be hard-pressed to take a bullet for.

Chapter Three

"There you go, mom," Cadman said, as he stood back to admire the shelves he finished attaching to the wall. "Now, you can load it up with your knick-knacks and free up the top of your dresser."

His seventy-three-year-old mother eyed the new shelves. "Maybe I should have had you put it on the other wall."

He grabbed a framed photo and placed it on the top shelf. "It's fine where it is." He was not about to redo it.

"Fine, but you'll stay for supper then."

Another hour would not hurt. She was not getting any younger. "I can do that."

"Good." With a cane in hand, she turned to exit the room. "We'll have leftover casserole."

Behind his mother's back, Cadman made a face. He hated her leftover casserole. His mother's casserole was a code word for surprise in a bowl. It consisted of all the leftover food she made during the week dumped into a casserole dish with cream of mushroom soup poured over the top.

With a resigned sigh, he said, "Oh, yummy." He'd had worse in his life. There'd been times during a mission with the Task Force when they had to forage for whatever was edible, and that meant he had eaten his fair share of worms, grubs, and termites over the years.

Thankfully, his mother's leftover casserole tasted better than those things. But barely.

"Can I help you with anything?" he asked when they reached the tiny kitchen.

"No, I can manage. I'll just use that microwave oven your brother got me for Christmas last year to warm it up."

At the mention of his brother Finn, Cadman asked, "How is that brother of mine?"

"If you ever called him, you would know."

Sigh. Why could she not just answer the question without having to make it sound as though he never spoke to his sibling? He talked to his brother at least twice a month. They were both busy men. Finn was a lawyer working for a firm that specialized in corporate matters.

His mother pulled the casserole out from the refrigerator, placed it into the microwave, and set the timer. "He's fine. So are his wife and my grandbabies."

As the casserole warmed in the microwave, she turned to say, "You know I love my grandbabies."

"Yep," he answered and thought, here it comes. Every time he visited his mother, it was the same conversation. She wanted him married, settled down, and actively adding to her list of grandchildren.

"Tomorrow's Valentine's Day, do you have someone special to celebrate it with?" she asked.

Strangely, the image of that lunatic manager Kasey E popped into his head.

Ridiculous! He did not even like the crazy bitch.

"No, mom. We've been over this. I'm not interested in having a wife and kids."

His mother removed the heated dish from the microwave and placed the contents on a plate before bringing it to him. "But if you had a wife, you wouldn't be lonely."

He shook his head. "I'm not lonely."

She brought her own plate to the table. “You went out and got yourself a dog, didn’t you?”

He almost choked. “I didn’t buy Mutt because I was lonely.”

“No?” How his mother could make a two-letter word sound like a sing-song, with a, I don’t believe you tone in her voice he would never know. “Then why would you want one?”

Frustrated, he blurted an answer before thinking it through, “Because I wanted some company at night when I’m home.”

“Because you’re lonely.”

Ugg. He was trying to be a good son. He’d come over to put up those shelves when he would have rather been home watching the television show Black Sheep Squadron. But no, he stood in a line for what seemed like forever, then was accused of stealing from that Attila-the-Hun reincarnation cashier Kasey E., - store manager. Now his mother was giving him the “You should be married” speech.

“Mom, I’m happy.”

“Don’t you like children?”

For the love of… Why was it when he told people he did not want children, they assumed he did not like them?

He loved kids, but he loved them better when they belonged to someone else.

Besides his brother’s two kids, there were seven children in this world he adored, and soon to be eight once Rosalinda gave birth to her baby, which should be any day now.

His brother had two children. And he was a surrogate uncle to six children that lived in North Dakota, belonging to his best friend, Colten Fisher, and his wife, Jacqueline. The other one lived in Paris, France, and he was the son of Rosalinda and Charles.

Even though he loved them all, he could not say he did not have a favorite. Colten's third child, Hunter, now eleven years old, impressed him the most.

Cadman believed Hunter's destiny lay in one of the military branches. At age ten, he already showed the potential to be a great asset to a group like Task Force Ghost. The kid was damn good at martial arts, having surpassed what the local instructors of the sport could teach him.

Colten had reached out to one of the top martial arts instructors in the world when Hunter turned eight. The sessions should have cost the Fishers a fortune, considering the instructor flew to North Dakota once a week for the private lessons. But when the teacher saw Hunter in action, the man charged only half his fee. He'd found the diamond in the rough others only dreamed of discovering.

Hunter also had an Eidetic memory, an ability to recall text, numbers, and patterns quickly. Not that Hunter was a genius, but to Cadman's thinking, the kid was close to it.

"Mom," Cadman said, taking a bite of the casserole, chewed, and swallowed. "Think of it this way. I'm saving you money. Fewer presents to buy at Christmas and birthdays."

His mother shook her head and knew her son was a lost cause. "So, you're telling me you're only going to give me a grand dog?"

He took another bite. "Yep. Mutt loves those Milk-Bone things. Especially those new beef-flavored ones. I'm sure he'll love you to death if you put a box under the tree for him in December."

Cadman pushed his plate away. "I'll help you clean up, then I've got to head home."

"I'll manage the cleanup. Not much in the way of dirty dishes with just the two of us," she told him. "You just make sure you visit sooner next time." She paused, looking up with an eye roll. "And bring my grand dog with you when you come."

He was grinning as he walked out the door.

It took him a little over a half-hour to drive from his mother's home in Woodhaven to his quiet street in Cottage City. It was dark by the time he pulled into the driveway, and his headlights caught the realtor sign next door, showing it now had a sold sticker on it. It looked as though he would have new neighbors, and he hoped they were not loud and obnoxious. He enjoyed city life, but he liked his quiet too.

As he unlocked and opened the front door of his house, Mutt leaped up and tried licking him in the face.

Cadman half laughed; half scolded. "Yeah, yeah. I'm happy to see you too." He took off his new vest and almost tossed it on the chair before he glanced at Mutt and thought better of it. There was no sense in leaving temptation out. Hell, he was still finding feathers around the house from the last vest the dog destroyed.

Mutt ran for the back door.

"Okay, okay," he told the dog as he followed the canine through the house. As he passed the phone in the kitchen, he noticed the message light was blinking on his answering machine.

He let the dog outside and into the fenced-in yard, then went back to the recorder and pushed play.

"Cadman!" It was Rosalinda's voice, but she was crying, and his heart clenched. Eleven years ago, the woman was subjected to unspeakable torture and rape. Despite the unimaginable pain and trauma, she proved her strength over the months it took for her body and mind to heal. After enduring such horrors, she did not deserve any further suffering. Had something happened to the baby? Her son? Charles?

Suddenly Rosalinda's voice took on a weird combination of laughing and crying. "Charles and I have a beautiful baby girl!"

Cadman reached for the nearest chair as his heart soared. He felt his own tears swell up in relief. Now he understood why the woman's voice was so emotional.

It was a cry of joy.

"You must come to see her!" Rosalinda's voice said. "Her name is Daniela. Daniela Elizabeth Geneviève Athenais Lafayette."

Cadman could not help his laughter. It was apparent the Lafayette's enjoyed saddling their children with long names.

They'd named their son Mason Richard Fernando Antoine Albert Lafayette.

"Cadman," He heard Charles Lafayette's voice now on the recorder. "Come as soon as you can. She is as beautiful as her mother!"

Suddenly he could hear eleven-year-old Mason's voice say, "I do not know if I like her, Uncle Cadman."

Cadman's roar of laughter joined the recorded amusement of the boy's parents.

When the message ended, he glanced at his watch and knew it was only 3:45 in the morning in Paris. He would not call them back until a more appropriate time. He did not want to disturb them if they were sleeping; there would be plenty of early morning wake-up calls from the new baby.

He would request time off as soon as possible and plan his trip to France to meet the newest addition of the Lafayette family.

Chapter Four

She could not believe she'd accused that man of shoplifting!

What on earth was wrong with her?

Kasey unlocked the door of her apartment, stepped inside, knowing the only reason she still had a job was because her dad loved her, and he owned the hardware store.

"Sure, daddy. I'll come back to Washington and help you out," she told him three months ago when he asked for her help, and she was looking for a new beginning.

More likely, she would get the store sued for slander and cost her dad the business he built up over the past thirty years.

Glancing at herself in the mirror, she scolded her reflection, "How could you do such a stupid thing?!"

Yes, dad had mentioned the increase in shoplifting at his store over the past year. And yes, she had only been trying to look out for the business, but when the man claimed he already owned the vest, she should have ended it there. But no. She questioned him like she was one of Charlie's Angels out to get the bad guy.

She was a nurse for god's sake, even if not employed as one. She had yet to decide if she wanted to go back to the demands of nursing since she left California to move back home. She'd seen enough trauma over the years to last a lifetime.

With her index finger, she poked her reflection in the mirror. "You're the reason men make up those dumb blond jokes!" she told herself.

She shook her head, knowing it was not true. But for the love of Peter, Paul, and Mary, what had she been thinking?

Closing her eyes, she took a deep breath and blew it out to calm herself. It had been a mistake. A silly, ridiculous blunder and it would not be the end of the world.

She hoped.

A meow from behind her had her smiling.

Turning, she saw her pure white, blue-eyed, Maine Coon cat standing in the doorway leading to the kitchen staring at her. "Hello, Dolly. Did you miss me?" Kasey cooed at her beloved pet, her upset forgotten as her cat slowly came forward, circling her legs as it purred.

With two hands, Kasey picked up the twenty-eight-pound fur ball and rubbed her face into its silky pelt.

"You're such a good girl. I know you do not like this small place, but it won't be long before you have the run of a larger area."

Placing Dolly back on the floor, Kasey walked into the kitchen. She opened the cupboard and reached for the dry cat food bag. The sound of kibble pouring from the bag into the half-empty cat dish had Dolly pouncing headlong for the dish as though she had been starving.

"Honestly, Dolly. There was still food in your dish. Maybe you need glasses?" Kasey chuckled at her own joke when a vision of her cat wearing eyeglasses popped into her head.

Moving into the living room, Kasey turned on the television and flipped through the channels, hoping to find something of interest to watch while she ate her dinner. She was glad to see Sanford and Son was on tonight. The comic relief was exactly what she needed to put that guy with the vest out of her mind.

Oh god, the look on that man's handsome face when she stood there, accusing him of stealing without witnessing it. He looked as though he swallowed a lemon!

And she had told him to have a wonderful day! Priceless.

She tried to find amusement at the whole situation and hoped the man could do the same.

Her phone rang before she could enter the kitchen to make herself a peanut butter and jelly sandwich or poured a bowl of cereal. Whichever, she was not in the mood to cook anything.

It was liberating not to have Richard around, demanding a hot meal after she had worked all day.

She should have divorced the son-of-a-bitch sooner.

Correction, she should have never married the son-of-a-bitch.

Richard assumed that because he was a man who earned more, it was her job to cook every night, despite her rotating hospital shifts. The narcissist believed that since he was a doctor who made enough to support them, she should happily abandon nursing to become his complacent little wife. His wealth meant nothing to her; she genuinely enjoyed working as a nurse and helping people.

What in the hell had she been thinking when she said yes to his proposal?

There had been more than one fight over her choice to continue working during the short six-month marriage.

"You're a woman!" Richard would scream. "You're supposed to stay at home, keep the house, and have babies."

Male chauvinist pig!

She had never been interested in having children. Now, at forty-five, starting a family was obviously out of the question.

They should have talked about that before they got married. In fact, they should have talked about a lot of things before planning a wedding. His charming personality had blindsided her, idiot that she was. He had showered her with attention from the first day, taking her on expensive dates to fancy restaurants, sporting events, and Hollywood glamorous

parties. She should have seen him for what he really was: a self-absorbed, arrogant, and manipulative man. Why hadn't she noticed his belief that men were superior to women while she was dating him?

"Because Richard is a conniving, manipulative ass, that's why," she said out loud. She could also admit it had been sexual hormones. She had been forty-four years old on the day she said, "I do." Her first marriage, his fifth. The fact he had been married several times before should have been a big clue she was making a mistake in hitching herself to him.

She had never planned to marry. From an early age, she knew she wanted to become a nurse and find adventure. At eighteen, she signed up with the Red Cross for training, and a year later, she found the adventure she'd been looking for when the Korean War began in 1950, and she was deployed overseas tending the wounded. After the Korean War ended, she returned to the United States, but her service wasn't over. In 1965, she left again for Vietnam when the Red Cross called for personnel to aid American combat troops there. Her service to the Red Cross finally ended seven years later in 1972, and she was more than ready to return stateside. The Red Cross officially withdrew its remaining personnel from Vietnam the following year in 1973, when the United States began withdrawing its fighting forces.

Following her service in Vietnam, she arrived at LAX and initially planned a short, week-long visit with friends to help her readjust to civilian life. That week rapidly extended into two, then three, weeks. Realizing her need for stability, she secured a hospital job and gradually began to build a permanent new life in California.

The job was her saving grace. She helped heal the sick, and somehow, they, in turn, soothed her soul. For almost two years, she worked side-by-side with the doctors without the fear she experienced during her deployment overseas. For a long time, the memories of Vietnam filled her nightmares with the fears of the real possibility she could have been shot at by the Viet Cong or been hit by a grenade.

Someone Like You

A year into her new nursing job, Richard Evans walked into the ER. He had the looks of a model and the ego of someone who knew they were good looking, though it had not been until after the wedding when arrogance broke through, and she realized she made a mistake when she married him.

She pushed Richard from her mind and answered the phone. "Hello?"

"Kasey, thank god!"

Of all the people, she thought as she looked at the receiver in her hand. Suddenly it felt like the phone had turned into a snake, which was possible since the voice coming through the wire belonged to one. Perhaps by thinking about him, she caused this to happen, but she could not believe her ex would dare call her up.

"Richard, what in the hell do you want?"

"Now, Kasey, don't be vulgar."

"I'm hanging up, Richard. We've been divorced for just over three months, and I certainly do not have to talk to you." With that statement, the hand she was holding the receiver with began the motion to disconnect.

"Kasey, wait!"

She heard his plea and hesitated.

Knowing she probably shouldn't, she put the receiver next to her ear once more. With a sigh, she asked, "What do you want, Richard?"

"I miss you. Honestly, Kasey, we can work things out. I love you, and you know you need me. I'm the best thing to have ever happened to you."

Was he kidding?

"Goodbye, Richard."

This time she hung up without a second thought. He probably was not happy with the alimony payments her lawyer had gotten the judge to award her. He would have to pay her half his salary until he retired, or she remarried.

If she was wise with her finances, she would have a sizable income for at least twenty years because she was not interested in ever remarrying.

Chapter Five

Four months later - June 1976.

Gone was the chilly winter. Spring arrived with average temperatures, giving Kasey ample time to complete the move into the new home she purchased in February. While waiting for the mild temperatures, she worked on painting each room in the two-bedroom house before moving in at the end of March.

Dolly loved the open space. The feline spent a week exploring each room, getting used to the new smells.

The Ranch Style, two-Bedroom, one-bathroom home, was small but larger than her apartment had been. There was a screened-in porch in the back, and the front porch had a beautiful railing that looked like fence posts, giving the space a charming appeal.

Kasey loved it. Richard would have hated it, which made her even happier to have purchased it with his money.

She did not want to think about Richard anymore. The man had been calling her every other week since February.

She was seriously considering sending him a muzzle. If that did not send a clear message, she could always change her phone number.

This was her weekend off. Today she planned to spend the day in the front yard planting flowers. A mixture of perennials that would have something blooming all summer long.

Working on a small patch of soil near her front door, she peered at the house next door. She hadn't met her new neighbors, and their schedule seemed mysterious. She figured they either kept unusual hours or were home exclusively during the long stretches she spent working at the hardware store.

Kasey occasionally saw a teenage girl walking a German Shepherd around the block. She assumed the girl lived there since she was the only one who exercised the dog, but Kasey had yet to introduce herself. However, she had also noticed a van occasionally pull up, taking the dog away for what seemed like a week or more before returning it. The sight made her feel sorry for the animal. Despite being a cat lover, she was developing a soft spot for the dog and couldn't help but wonder about its owners. If they weren't able to care for the creature, why had they acquired it?

She almost had the urge to lie in wait for the owners and give them a lecture on how to take care of their dog but changed her mind each time the thought occurred. It was not as though the dog appeared mistreated. And she did not know what reasons the owners had for having the dog passed from one person to the other, so she held her peace and minded her own business.

Sitting back on her heels, she examined her handy work and smiled. Her yard would be gorgeous this summer when all those flowers bloomed.

Deciding she needed a break and a glass of refreshing lemonade; she stood up and walked into the house to do just that.

Her front door closed just as a black Firebird pulled into the driveway next door. Cadman got out of the vehicle and headed up the short walkway to his own home.

These past four months had been a whirlwind of events. Cadman spent a month in France with the Lafayette's, then returned to the States only to receive word that a criminal he'd been tracking for eleven years was rumored to be in Columbia. He quickly packed his bags, called the emergency dog sitters for Mutt, and headed down to the jungles of South America. Pierre Bellefeuille, wanted by authorities in both America and France for heinous crimes, was the one man Cadman wanted to see behind bars, if not dead, more than anything. This was a personal quest that began the day Bellefeuille kidnapped, tortured, and raped

Rosalinda, leaving her nearly dead before her rescue. If Cadman accomplished one thing before his retirement, it would be putting a bullet in Bellefeuille's head. Unfortunately, the trip was a waste of time. For ten days, Cadman risked his life questioning people in an area ruled by four major drug trafficking cartels, knowing too many questions could get him killed. He managed to stay off the cartel's radar, but if Bellefeuille had been there, he had disappeared into the wind before Cadman could find his whereabouts.

Cadman had been beyond disappointed.

Thinking about Bellefeuille also brought about images of Mason Lafayette. As far as the world knew, Charles was the boy's father, but Pierre was the biological one. Charles loved Mason as though he were his own blood, but Cadman wondered how much longer they could keep the truth of his parentage a secret. It had been apparent during this last visit to Paris, when he met baby Daniela, that Mason was developing Pierre's features. The boy's black hair and green eyes, inherited from Rosalinda, kept him from being a mirror image, but his looks had Pierre Bellefeuille written all over them. People would begin wondering sooner rather than later if Charles was, in fact, the boy's real father, if they hadn't quietly done so already. The story of the kidnapping had been a major international news story at the time.

After Columbia, there had been three hostage situations Cadman led his team into. Two of the ops had been successful, one had not, and Cadman was sorry for it.

He would not, could not think of those they had lost.

Now, as he found the key to his house, he sighed with pleasure. It was great to be home. It was not unusual for him to be gone for a week here, and a week there, when situations arrived that required his team, but this stretch of absence from home had been grueling. After being in Paris for that month, then South America, it felt as though every lunatic in the world had begun some uprising or another. It had kept him away longer than he would have liked.

As Cadman opened his front door, he welcomed Mutt's exuberant greeting, glad the dog remembered him. He was thankful that the dog service brought the animal back home before he arrived. It was kind of nice to have someone waiting for you, even if that someone had four legs.

Laughing as the dog licked, panted, and barked with excitement, Cadman said, "I missed you too, boy."

They wrestled together on the living room floor, knocking over a vase and a lamp, which both promptly broke into pieces, but Cadman did not care. It felt good to be home, and he was sorry he had to use the unique dog service more often than usual while he'd been away. He could not help the fact his job required the absence. When he'd not known how long his delay in returning home would be, he had not wanted Mutt to become lonely, nor could he expect Becky to see to the dog's needs during the night.

He would have to give Becky a big tip for always being willing to help in a pinch.

Mutt rushed for the back door, Cadman stood up and let the dog out, then began cleaning up the mess they had made.

As he glanced out the kitchen window, he remembered he had new neighbors. Perhaps tomorrow, he would go over there and introduce himself to them. After all this time, they probably thought he was not a friendly person.

Chapter Six

Kasey walked out the front door, ready to work more on her flower garden, and froze.

She could not believe it! There was a dog busy digging up everything she had planted that morning!

"Hey, you stupid mutt!" she yelled, recognizing the beast. She had seen it often enough when it was out for its walks. She knew damn well which house on the block the thing belonged to.

Hearing his name, Mutt gleefully bounced toward her. Tail wagging, body swaying, he approached her with his tongue hanging out, and a look on his face that Kasey would have sworn was a smile if she was not madder than a hornet.

"Someone's going to pay for that," she declared, reaching for Mutt's collar without second-guessing if the animal would bite.

Taking a firm grip on the collar, seeing the Pontiac Firebird in the driveway, she knew she was about to meet at least one of her neighbors for the first time and knew it was not promising to be a pleasant conversation.

Mutt, oblivious to having done anything wrong, walked along with his new friend as though there was nothing unusual about a stranger hanging onto his collar.

Kasey marched up the steps to the house next door and pounded on the door with enough force the wood vibrated.

It swung open as he said, "Good God, what's the-"

They stared at each other for a beat. Recognition was instant, and simultaneously they exclaimed, "You!"

Neither of them could believe they were seeing the other.

Cadman could not help himself. The first one to say something, he told her, "If you expect me to show you the receipt for the Firebird, you can forget it."

To his satisfaction, her face went scarlet.

"Is this your damn dog?" she snarled back.

Cadman's eyes glanced down, saw Mutt was full of dirt. He looked Kasey in the eyes and said, "I don't have the receipt for him, so I guess I could claim no."

The nerve of him. "Is this your house?" she questioned instead. Please, please, don't let him be my neighbor.

"Do you want to see the title and proof of insurance?"

She wanted to kick him.

"Your dog," she said the word as though it was the most horrible thing to ever roll off her tongue, "dug up my flower garden! I just spent two hours planting it, and he destroyed it in less than five minutes!"

Cadman glanced back down at Mutt, scowled, and wondered how the canine had gotten itself out from the fenced-in backyard. Cadman could not blame Kasey E. - manager for being a mite upset, and he could see by the evidence of Mutt's filthy fur there had been a crime.

"Where do you live?" he suspected he knew the answer, but that did not prevent him from hoping she would not say….

"Next door."

He sighed, pinched the bridge of his nose. He would have to accept it. What else could he do? "Look, I'm sorry." He got his voice to a conversational level. "My backyard is fenced in. I don't know how he got out. If you give me ten minutes to change into some working clothes, I'll come over and help you replant your flowers."

Kasey blinked. She had not expected that. She had expected to have an apology at most. Maybe an offer to pay for some of the damage, but—he was offering to help replant the flowers? "Umm, okay?"

He reached out, took hold of the dog's collar. "Come on, Mutt. You've been a bad dog."

It might have been in the tone but damned if the dog didn't stop wagging his tail, and his head went down as Kasey released her hold and watched him slowly walk into the house like a child who knew they were about to be scolded.

Damn it, now she felt sorry for the dog. "What's his name?" she heard herself ask.

"Mutt."

"You named him, Mutt?"

Cadman shrugged. "Not very original, I know. I couldn't think of anything else." He began to close the door. "Like I said, I'll change and be over in about ten minutes."

The door closed in her face, but she did not notice. She was too stunned that he was her neighbor, and that he would help her with replanting the flowers.

Flowers. She had never met a man who would be willing to do such a thing.

Well, her father would if mom nagged him long enough, and her brother, Malcolm, could have his arm twisted, but this guy had offered to help in less than a heartbeat.

She had to admire at least that about him.

True to his word, ten minutes later, Kasey watched her neighbor walking toward her. He had changed into a pair of worn and faded jeans that seemed to fit him like a glove, and she felt her mouth go dry. Now that she was not angry with him, nor accusing him of shoplifting, she could

admit to herself he was a handsome man. He had medium brown hair that had some gray peeking through, as did the short beard covering his jaw and the mustache above his lip. His short-sleeved t-shirt stretched over a broad, muscular chest as though it struggled to contain the width of the pecs.

It did not take a genius to figure out the man was used to physical labor.

He approached, stuck out his hand. “The names Cadman. Cadman Benson. Figured we should probably know each other’s names.”

She tore her eyes away from that mouthwatering chest and looked up into those hazel eyes of his that reminded her of autumn tones, brown with specs of gold.

“Umm,” she shook his hand. “Kasey. Kasey Evans.”

His smile revealed a dimple she found adorable as hell.

His eyes scanned the damage Mutt had caused, winced. “Sorry about Mutt. I checked the backyard. It looks like the back gate was left open from the last time he had a walk.”

Kasey nodded, handed him a hoe. “I hope you won’t be too hard on your daughter for being careless.”

Cadman looked at her. Raised a brow in question. “I don’t have a daughter.”

She tried not to let her shock show through. That young teenager she had seen walking Mutt could not possibly be his girlfriend.

Closing her eyes, she prayed she did not live next door to a pervert.

Then she laughed. Of course the girl was probably a relative.

“I’m sorry, I meant your niece.”

He shook his head. “Who, and what, are you talking about? My nieces are five years old.”

Color shot up her face. Obviously, he had a much too young girlfriend. "I've seen a teenager walking Mutt…" she trailed off.

He stared at her for a beat, then narrowed his eyes. He had an idea she was assuming there was something between himself and Becky. "Are you naturally suspicious of everyone, or is it just me you like to accuse of wrongdoing?" He took the hoe from her and began using it with angry motions as he leveled a patch of dirt, dug a hole, and plopped one flower Mutt had dug up into the crevice.

The sooner they got this job done, the sooner he could be away from the slanderer.

Fuck it, he decided. It was time to set this woman straight. He spun toward her so fast she almost yelped. "For your information, miss falsehood, the girl's name is Becky. I've hired her to walk Mutt when I can't, which is often because of my job." He threw the hoe down. Three angry steps brought him directly into Kasey's space. There was not more than an inch between them as he lowered his face toward hers and shouted, "Do I make myself clear?"

Kasey's eyes went huge. She had heard no one that authoritative since her days with the Red Cross in Vietnam, and she had the incredible urge to salute.

Tears formed in her eyes. He had a right to his anger. She had done nothing to endear herself to him, and now all she wanted to do was curl up into a ball and cry. Not for herself, but for her treatment of him.

"Fucking A, don't you dare cry!" he snapped.

"I won't," she sniffed, then did just that.

Cadman stepped back as though he'd unleashed an inferno. Good god, what had he done? Yes, the woman drove him crazy, and yes, her assumption had pissed him off, but she was not one of his team members. He'd barked at her as though she were a recruit. His mother would have his head if she knew he had spoken to a woman like that.

He raked his hands through his hair in frustration. “Hey, I’m sorry.”

Well, Jesus H. Christ, that only made her cry harder.

Kasey swiped at her tears. “I’m the one who should tell you I’m sorry!” she cried. “I don’t know what’s wrong with me. I don’t even know you! How could I blunder so badly? I’m really not a mean person.”

Awkwardly, he patted her arm in a feeble attempt to comfort her.

“Perhaps we could work on putting these flowers back in their holes?” he said, wanting to be away from this crazy woman. “A little hard work can help set the mind at ease. Let’s just forget this whole thing, do the job, and get it done.”

She sniffed. “Okay.”

Cadman retrieved the hoe she had handed him earlier. Turning his back on her, he began smoothing dirt, gathering the displaced flowers, and replanting them as he went. He mostly ignored his neighbor. She did not seem to want to talk while they worked, which was okay with him. He was not in the mood for conversation.

They finished what had taken Kasey two hours that morning to do in less than thirty minutes.

Standing back, they admired their handy work.

“It will look nice this summer when it’s in bloom,” Cadman said, wiping his hands on the legs of his jeans, figuring he could be civil enough to at least admit that truth.

She nodded. “Thank you for helping.”

He sighed. “It was the least I could do since it was my dumb dog who made the mess.” He saw the seven dozen or so trays of flowers sitting on her porch waiting to be planted. She still had a lot of work ahead of her, and he told himself that was her problem.

Opening his mouth to tell her goodbye, have a nice day, and leave me the hell alone, he was shocked when the words, "I can help with those," popped out instead.

When had he become a glutton for punishment? he wondered as he marveled at himself for having made the offer. His job here was done. There was no need to linger.

She stared at him as though she could not fathom he'd offered to help her out farther.

"Umm," she licked her lips, and his eyes followed its path. "I appreciate the offer, but I'm sure you have other things you were planning to do today."

She handed the perfect opportunity to him to back out of his offer to help, and yet he told her, "My plans can wait a little longer." He was only going to visit his mother this afternoon to see if she needed help with anything. And maybe take her to the grocery store if the woman he and his brother hired to check in on her twice a week had forgotten to pick her up an item.

Kasey shrugged. "All right. I won't say no to free labor." She gestured toward the porch. "I have some rose bushes I was going to put in, too. So, if you're handy with a shovel, I'll put you to work."

"Not a problem," he said and wondered why he was willing to break his back for her. But digging a couple of holes in the ground would not strain him.

Then she said, "I have eight of them. They are going on that side of the house." She pointed toward the area in front of her living room window.

"Eight?" Brother. He sure as hell needed to learn to keep his damn mouth shut.

She laughed. "Oh god, the look on your face! I'm sorry. I know I shouldn't be pushing my luck, and I have no right to tease you, but I

couldn't resist." She shook her head. "I do not have any roses bushes to plant. Only flowers."

Cadman stared at her for a beat. He had not expected her humor after what had happened earlier.

"None?" he asked and managed to sound disappointed.

Kasey shook her head.

"Well, damn. I was so looking forward to breaking my back."

Her wide as Texas smile had his heart skipping a beat. "Lier," she said.

A corner of his mouth twitched. "Okay, maybe a little. Let's get those flowers planted and move on with our lives."

Kasey was not sure if he was mad at her or relieved, but it was apparent he was still willing to help her, as long as they did it quickly, and they could go back to their separate lives. At least they could be civil neighbors, and not at each other's throats.

That was something to be thankful for.

Chapter Seven

Monday morning, Cadman walked into his office, wondering what this week would bring and hoped things would be quiet. It would mean no one was trying to overthrow someone, and no one was threatening to bomb something. Contrary to what people around him thought, he did not live for danger. He would rather make it to his grave as an old man, rather than having some bullet put him there. But he was not afraid of dying if it meant saving someone else's life.

"Good morning, sir," his secretary said. The man stood up from behind his desk, gave Cadman a quick salute, then handed him a stack of mail. "I have your schedule for the week on your desk. The coffee is fresh if you would like me to bring you some, and Mr. Wade called. He asked me to have you call him right away."

Cadman gave a half-hearted salute back to his secretary. He had requested long ago for his office to operate in an informal manner, but his secretary was the type to strictly follow rules, and Cadman knew he wouldn't change. "Thanks, Mark. Just hold off on any calls for now, unless it's from my boss."

"Yes, sir. The president gets top priority."

Cadman walked into his office, closed the door. He supposed he might as well call Mr. Wade, although that was not the man's real name. The guy was an informant. A snitch who kept his eyes and ears open for activity the law might want to know about. Usually, the information was more useful to the local authorities. If what the man had to say was along those lines, Cadman would send him to the proper channel.

Once in a while though, the information was useful to Task Force Ghost. The informant's name was actually Peter Ennis, and Cadman could not fault the man for using an alias. It would be hell to have a name that sounded like penis. The man's parents must have thought it

was a sick joke to name him Peter on top of it. Any other first initial other than P would have been preferable, Cadman was sure.

Cadman sat down at his desk, reached for the phone, and dialed Mr. Wade's number. There was no guarantee the man would be near the phone booth he used for telephone conversations. And there was always a chance some other homeless person would pick up the call.

The phone rang eight times before it was answered.

"Hello?"

"I'm looking for Mr. Wade."

"Do you know the code?"

Cadman rolled his eyes and hated having to recite Wade's, haha, secretive verse. But Cadman also knew the game, and so he said, "A horse! A horse! My kingdom for a horse!"

God, he hated horses more than ever, having to say that.

"And?" the voice on the other side of the line prompted.

"Shakespeare. Richard III Act 5, Scene 4."

"Mr. Benson!" Mr. Wade wheezed in a heavy smoker's voice. "I have information I think would interest you. Meet me at our usual spot and bring the package."

Package being code for money. Nothing was free. If Cadman wanted the info Wade had, he would have to pay for it before discovering if it was useful or not. It was Wade's way of getting extra money because if Cadman was not interested, he would sell it to the cops.

Cadman glanced at his watch. "I can make it there in an hour."

"Fine. Fine." And Wade hung up without a goodbye.

Cadman clicked the intercom button and told his secretary, "Coffee." He'd need the caffeine to make it through the substantial backlog on his desk and began meticulously reviewing his schedule for the day and flipping through the stacks of classified reports that had accumulated over the past few days.

Thank God nothing looked as though he needed to put together a team soon.

When Mark brought the mug of coffee in, steaming hot and black as sin, Cadman told him, “I need you to bring me some cash from the informant fund.”

“How much would you like, sir?”

“I’m not giving the weasel over fifty bucks, but I’ll try to keep it at twenty, so you might as well bring me one hundred on the off chance he’s got something to say.”

“Yes, sir.”

There was that damn salute again.

Mark exited the office, and Cadman went back to scanning files. By the time his secretary brought the cash, Cadman noted he had only fifteen minutes to reach the rendezvous point. He knew, however, that Wade would wait regardless of his tardiness; the prospect of receiving money to spend on drugs was a powerful incentive to a junkie.

Cadman hated the fact he knew what Wade would spend the money on, but that was out of his control.

* * *

As Kasey walked along the sidewalk, she began shifting through the stack of mail she was carrying to the box; conducting a quick inspection to ensure her dad, bless his distracted heart, had remembered to put stamps on every single piece that required postage.

Today was lovely. The sun was warm on her face as she walked, the golden rays caressing her skin with a gentle touch. She couldn't help but smile as she took in the sights and sounds of the bustling city streets, the aroma of fresh flowers and hot coffee wafting through the air.

Strolling along the familiar street, she couldn't suppress the feeling of absolute contentment. She cherished the simple act of walking along a quiet sidewalk, constantly reminding herself how glad she was to be home in D.C., far removed from the constant danger and trauma of overseas service.

Upon reaching the mailbox she confirmed, once again, that all the envelopes had stamps on them, then slid them through the slot.

Kasey started to pivot back toward the hardware store when she spotted two men loitering in the alleyway. They weren't making much effort to hide, only partially obscured by the building's overgrown landscaping. She was about to dismiss them, but something about the posture of one figure pulled her up short, and when recognition dawned, she stood rooted in place.

Cadman Benson was there, speaking to what appeared to be a homeless man. As she watched, it looked as though the unkempt man was looking nervously about as he reached into the inside of his jacket and pulled out a small bag. Cadman handed him something that from this distance, Kasey thought was cash.

Oh. My. God! Kasey tried not to jump to conclusions. Lord knew she'd already falsely accused her neighbor of a crime once, but she was sure she'd just witnessed her neighbor purchase drugs! She would never have suspected Cadman was a junkie.

Should she intervene? Report this to the authorities? Kasey knew she shouldn't get involved, but she couldn't stand by and watch as her neighbor destroyed himself eather!

Perhaps this was his first time using, and he didn't grasp how quickly a person could get hooked. She'd seen it before, the young and naïve falling prey to the temptations of drugs, chasing a high that would ultimately lead to their downfall. She was torn between ignoring this or talking to him about it. But technically, it was not her place to counsel him.

It startled her when she noticed Cadman and the man had parted ways, and her neighbor was walking this way. Toward her!

She couldn't face him. Not now. Not without knowing what to say to him about his drug use and her feet got her moving in the opposite direction, but not before he saw her.

"Hey, Kasey!" Cadman called out in greeting.

Shit. Shit. She could not very well be rude as much as she wanted to.

She turned around; plastered a smile on her face. "Oh, hi!" she exclaimed. Her voice came out sounding like a high-pitched squeak.

"Are you okay?" he asked, and she flushed.

"Fine!" That damn squeak again.

She cleared her throat. "It sure turned into a beautiful day. What brings you to this neck of the woods?"

"I had some business to attend to."

Kasey glanced over his shoulder at the alleyway. "Oh?"

"Anyway, I'm about to head back to work. I saw you and thought I would say hello."

"Wasn't that nice of you?"

"By the way, I fixed the gate in the backyard. It shuts on its own now if someone forgets to close it. At least now my dog won't be getting high from destroying your flower garden again."

Why did he have to refer to Mutt getting a buzz from digging in her garden when obviously he was planning on getting a buzz himself?

"Are you sure you're okay? You look a little pale."

She waved a hand. "I'm fine. Thank you again for helping me replant my flowers." She glanced at her watch without truly looking at the time. "Oh my, I'm late for an appointment. Got to run!"

Cadman watched her spin away, and he shook his head. His neighbor ranked right up there with the unexplainable.

It took him a minute to realize he was still watching her walking away from him, and enjoying the sway of her hips, and those killer calves of hers visible due to the knee-length dress she wore.

He shook himself, wondering what had gotten into him. He certainly did not want to find anything about his neighbor sexy. It was bad enough she was so damn pretty.

Shaking it off, he made his way to his Firebird. Once inside, he pulled out the baggy he'd gotten from Mr. Ward. He examined the ancient coin and wondered if it really was part of a smuggling operation that was financing a drug cartel in Mexico. It was more likely something he should turn over to drug enforcement guys, but he was not quite sure.

He started the car's engine, pulled away from the curb, and pondered the question all the way to his office.

Chapter Eight

That evening, Kasey paced her living room, obsessing over what she witnessed that morning in the alley.

Her cat sat in the doorway to the kitchen, watching her.

"I don't know what to do," Kasey said out loud, and her cat meowed.

"I know it's none of my business, but I was a nurse for god's sake," she told her cat. "I've seen what drugs do to a person, and it isn't pretty." The thought of her handsome neighbor transforming before her eyes, from a man who oozed sex appeal, to someone who no longer maintained their appearance because of drugs, made her ill.

Was he a pill popper? Did he snort cocaine? Inject heroin into his veins?

Thinking about it made her feel sick.

She went to her dining room, moved aside the curtain to peek at her neighbor's house, then dropped the cloth as though it caught fire when she realized what she was doing. Spying like some nosey old lady with nothing else to do with their time than keep track of what others were doing.

Her telephone rang, and she was glad for the distraction. Until she heard the voice on the line and wanted to scream. Of course, it had to be her ex-husband. His harassment was becoming tedious.

"Kasey, darling. How are you?"

"Oh, I'm doing great. I'm just sitting here polishing my gun." Her sarcasm was thick.

He had the nerve to tsk, and obviously, he was ignoring the implication she wanted to shoot him, figuratively as the threat had been. "You sound stressed. Are you taking care of yourself?"

"Richard, we both know you did not call to ask about my health."

"Dear Kasey, I cannot understand why you can't believe I'm concerned about your wellbeing. I do love you, you know. What can I do to help you see that?"

She laughed, knowing Richard only wanted her back because she'd left him. She wounded his ego when she'd done that. "Stop calling me, Richard. Goodbye."

At least she managed not to slam the receiver down when she disconnected. Perhaps one day, she would figure out a way to get him to stop calling her, but in the meantime, it was hard not to want to pull out her hair and scream at him.

He would probably like that if he knew he could ruffle her feathers and vowed to try harder not to feed his desire to see her upset.

When her phone rang again, not five minutes later, she debated with herself if she wanted to answer it. She had no way of knowing if it was Richard continuing with whatever game he was playing, but she was not a coward either.

She answered the phone, trying to keep the annoyance out of her tone.

"Hey, Kasey. What's shaking?" asked the voice on the other line once she'd said hello.

Relieved to hear a friend's voice instead of her ex's, Kasey smiled. "Hi, Sandy. How are you? Gosh, we haven't talked for a while."

"I know. That's why I called. I was wondering if you could do lunch tomorrow? Down at the Pier? We haven't been to our favorite restaurant down there in forever, and we could catch up on each other."

"That sounds like fun, though it would have to be a later lunch. Around two, if that would work for you? I can get away from the hardware store for a little while at that time of day."

"Sound's perfect. I'll see you at two tomorrow."

This time when Kasey hung up the phone, there was a smile on her face. Sandy was an old friend from high school, and she was looking forward to the visit. Maybe she could mention to Sandy what she saw her neighbor doing in the ally and ask for advice. The woman was psychiatrist, and the last time Kasey heard, worked with the police.

Kasey honestly did not want to see Cadman Benson destroy himself over drugs.

She decided to read for a little while before heading to bed. She needed the distraction of a good book to keep her mind from running wild with concerns that were not genuinely her business. Yet, that internal urge, the healer in her, persisted, tempting her to intervene and help Cadman overcome his addiction.

Selecting the fiction book she purchased last week, Saving the Queen, by William F. Buckley, she curled up on her couch to start the novel. One that apparently sends a CIA agent to Britain to identify a security leak.

To Kasey, this promised to be a wonderful spy thriller.

She read until midnight. With a yawn, she set the book down and began moving through her house to turn off lights and make sure she locked her doors.

As she reached her bedroom, she heard a car door slam, and because she had more curiosity than her cat, Kasey moved to her dining-room window and cautiously pulled the curtain back enough to see what was going on next door at Cadman's house at this hour of the night.

A beat-up black van was parked in Cadman's driveway, and the driver was approaching the front door. Kasey watched as her neighbor opened the door just before the visitor could knock. As the two conversed, Kasey placed her hand over her mouth, muffling a gasp of shock when the visitor suddenly pulled what looked like a gun from inside his coat.

When the person handed it to Cadman, Kasey relaxed because obviously, the person's intent had not been to shoot her neighbor. But she

continued to watch as Cadman, and the visitor stepped off the porch and headed for the back of the decrepit-looking van.

The person Kasey assumed was the driver opened the black van's rear doors, and Cadman immediately leaned inside. Kasey watched with fascinated horror as he dragged someone halfway out of the vehicle. Obscured by the shadows, she couldn't determine the figure's gender—it was too dark to make out anything but a vague outline. Then, with terrifying suddenness, and from Kasey's point of view, Cadman punched the figure in the face and shoved the body back into the van.

And Cadman laughed and patted the driver of the vehicle on the back!

Oh, my god! Oh my god! Kasey's mind screamed, and she rushed to the phone. She was going to call the police. She was not imagining things! It was apparent her neighbor was involved with something illegal.

And she had blatantly walked up to his door the other day and confronted him about his dog. She was lucky he had not shot her! On top of that, she'd cried over her treatment of him when now she knew she had not been wrong to suspect him of shoplifting! The law probably wanted him.

With righteous anger, Kasey dialed the number for the authorities. The second someone at the police station answered her call, she explained what she witnessed. She gave them Cadman's address but did not volunteer the fact he lived right next door to her. She wanted to remain anonymous. She'd read enough spy thrillers to know that somehow or other, the person who snitched wound up dead, and she had no intention of having someone drag her body from the river!

When she finished explaining, the officer asked, "Excuse me. What did you say the address was?"

She repeated it slowly to make sure the person could understand.

There was a long pause, then a cough. "Ma'am. With all due respect, I'm sure it was your vision playing tricks on you. That neighborhood is

pretty dark at night, and the streetlight can cast shadows. Sometimes things appear to be what they are not. You have nothing to worry about."

Kasey looked at the receiver as though she could not comprehend what it was. Was this man joking? She knew what she'd seen. Surely, she dialed the wrong number. What else could explain the person on the other end of the line not taking her information seriously?

"Is this the police department?"

"Yes, ma'am."

Well, that was not proof he was telling the truth. "What's your name and badge number?"

"Officer Jerry Fuhrmann," came the reply, and he rattled off a sequence of numbers.

"I'm hanging up and calling the real police."

"Yes, ma'am." Was that a laugh she heard in his voice?

Kasey hung up and redialed, making sure that this time, she dialed the right number.

"Police department, Officer Jerry Fuhrmann speaking."

Obviously, she had stepped through some weird vortex where the police no longer took their citizens seriously. "Never mind," she said. What was the point?

"Ma'am, if you would give me your name and address-"

She was not that stupid. If she did that, she would probably wind up in the back of some van, too. "Forget it," she said and hung up the phone.

Now what? She had begun to believe Cadman Benson was a nice man when he offered to help replant her flowers without complaint. And he'd been willing to dig holes for the non-existent rose bushes. She had even been considering inviting him to dinner some night as a way to say thank you.

Well, that idea sure as hell would not be expedited.

The cat meowed and was looking at her as though she'd lost her mind.

"All right! I'll go to bed," she told the cat, "But you better attack anyone who tries to come in here."

Who was she kidding? Her cat was more likely to make friends with any intruder.

Maybe in the morning, Kasey decided, she would have a better idea of what her next course of action would be. Perhaps she should call the FBI? But she would wait until the morning when she was rested and calmer.

In her house, as she switched off the light on the bedside table, Cadman was answering the phone in his own bedroom.

God, he hoped it was not a call to action. His eyes were tired, and so was his body.

"Yeah?" he snapped into the phone.

"Viper?"

"Yep." It was rarely anyone used his code name, so at least he knew this was not a random call.

"This is Officer Jerry Fuhrmann with the DC police department. I just wanted you to know we got an anonymous tip of some suspicious activity at your place tonight."

Cadman did not find the fact officer knew his code name unusual. The police force was not privy to what Cadman really did for the President of the United States, but they were all aware he had top clearance from the highest government official. Sometimes he worked closely with them if something they were working on lead to someone of interest to Task Force Ghost, although those times were rare.

"What do you mean? Nothing happened here tonight." He did not consider Daryl stopping by to give him that prop gun for Roy Alcorn's retirement party tomorrow night out of the norm.

Without question there were times a team member would stop by to give him an update if they felt he needed to be apprised of a situation immediately rather than wait until the morning, although that was unusual. He tried to keep his private life separate from the job. But he had wanted that prop in his hands tonight so he could drop it off at the bakery first thing in the morning. The team were all going to tease Roy about his inability to hit the broadside of a barn, and the fake gun was going on top of the cake.

"The report said you punched someone being held against their will in the back of a van."

Cadman lay in his bed, looking at the ceiling as he absorbed that bit of news. "I have no idea- "

When he realized why whoever made the report assumed the worst, he broke out in hearty laughter. He could understand how someone out walking their dog, if that was what the anonymous caller had been doing, could have assumed the worst.

Through fits of laughter, he explained to the officer what had been in the van. The conversation ended with the officer joining in on the merriment.

Chapter Nine

The next morning, after feeding her cat and having her own breakfast, Kasey headed for her Plymouth Roadrunner parked in her driveway. She was halfway to the driver's door when she saw Cadman Benson and his dog jogging up the sidewalk.

She quickened her pace, hoping to be able to slip into her car and go unnoticed by her neighbor. If she could avoid conversation with the man, her stress level would not elevate.

Even the goddamn FBI had not taken her phone call to them this morning seriously. They told her they appreciated her trying to be a good citizen, but they were sure she had nothing to worry about.

She lived next to a psychopath and had nothing to worry about?!

Apparently, the world had gone insane. At this point, Kasey was glad she hadn't bothered to tell the authorities about her ex-husband's harassment. No one would take that seriously, either.

"Kasey!"

Shit. She could not understand why Cadman was suddenly being the friendly neighbor. This was the second time, since he helped her plant those flowers, he greeted her as though they were friends.

And God damn it, why did he have to be so damn good looking? Even in those loose-fitting cotton jogging pants, and wearing another t-shirt advertising somewhere called Medora, she felt an attraction toward him.

No wonder she hadn't recognized Richard's narcissism when they dated. Apparently, she was a magnet for psychotic men.

Cadman jogged up to her just as she reached for the handle of her car. His dog danced circles around her legs.

“Oh!” she said breathlessly, trying to hide her nervousness. “My goodness, you’re up bright and early.”

He grinned at her, his mind calculating the best way to approach his suspicion. He needed to figure out exactly how to question her about the police call he received last night and the one from the FBI call this morning. Who else would accuse him of wrongdoing but the woman who had already accused him of shoplifting and happened to live right next door?

During his jog with Mutt, he went through last night in his head. He was trying to figure out who could have possibly witnessed Daryl at his door and presumed to know what was going on and alerted the authorities.

Kasey Evans had been the first and only culprit to go on his list of suspects.

He so wanted to make her sweat. It was apparent she was hell-bent on thinking the worst of him. It pissed him off enough to want to toy with her.

“Same goes, as I see you’re up early, too. I would think you would want to sleep in because of the disturbance last night.”

Her eyes were the only thing that gave her away. Cadman gave her credit for keeping her face a blank mask. “Disturbance?” her voice squeaked, and it gave him so much satisfaction he almost laughed. “What do you mean?”

“I’m sure you know. I had a late-night visitor.”

Hand going to her throat, she said, “Did you?”

He wondered if her face coloring could go any paler. “I did.” He took a step closer, crowding her space. “A friend of mine stopped by to drop something off for me. A fake gun we’re using as a decoration for a cake for a retirement party we are having tonight. The person retiring isn’t the best of shots, and we’re going to razz him about it. You know,” he

leaned in until his lips were next to her ear, and he whispered slowly, "It's a guy thing."

The warmth of his breath sent a shiver down her spine that, much to her dismay, was not because she was afraid.

When she realized he was telling her the gun she'd seen last night was not real, she stepped back and gasped, "It sure as hell looked real!"

He backed up and laughed. She just admitted she had indeed witnessed the whole thing.

His amusement at her expense had her hackles rising. "I'm glad you found that funny," she huffed.

"Oh, I do. I do indeed, although I shouldn't because for whatever reason you seem to have singled me out to think the worst of. And here I had been nice enough to help you replant your flowers without complaining about it, and yet here I am, on the receiving end of your suspicious mind. Again."

"You're right! But what was I supposed to think? Had it been a real gun, and the man shot you, wouldn't have you expected me to call the police then?"

Jerk.

"Probably," he admitted, "But that didn't happen."

Kasey thought that over. No crime was committed. Nor was there a law that said he could not own a gun. But that hadn't been the reason she called the police. She had seen the outline of a person in the back of that van. And she witnessed with her own eyes the man before her hit the person.

The fact she saw his violence should have caused her to clam up and keep her mouth shut yet, she forged ahead by saying, "Then who was in the back of that van, Mr. Benson? I witnessed you punch the person. For all I know, they need medical help."

He stared at her. Damn, she had a backbone. Although he hated her, he had to admire that aspect of her. If she genuinely expected him capable of violence, she should be leery of bringing that up.

"I hurt no one."

"I saw," she raised her voice, "you do it!"

"You saw me punch a sex doll." Seeing her face turn redder than a beet gave him so much pleasure. "It, too, is for my friend's party tonight."

"I… I… " she had no words.

"I honestly do not know what I have done to warrant your need to slander me, but it needs to stop."

"I… I…" God! "Wouldn't have you done the same thing if you'd been in my place?"

"No. No gun was not fired. And you only saw an outline of something you assumed was a person. You had no facts, but that didn't stop you from assuming the worst."

"Mr. Benson, I am so sorry!" she felt the tears coming and swept them away. What was wrong with her? She'd never been a person to jump to conclusions, but she'd been doing it since the moment she met him.

"I've heard that before," he said. "I'm sure you'll find something else to accuse me of before the day is through. Now, if you'll excuse me, I need to get ready to go to work." He spun around, called for Mutt, who was busy peeing on Kasey's flowers, and the pair jogged away.

Kasey watched as he disappeared into his house and closed the door. She did not understand how she could ever mend this rift she'd caused.

She closed her eyes and took a deep breath to clear her mind.

Wait a minute.

Her eyes popped back open, then narrowed as she watched Cadman disappear into his house. How had he known she had called anyone at all, least of all what she tried to report to the authorities?

She tried very hard not to jump to any conclusions, but she wondered if he'd bugged her phone.

"Stop it!" she told herself. Cadman Benson would have no reason to listen in on her conversations. But the question bothered her throughout the day.

* * *

As they sat, enjoying the bustling atmosphere and the ocean breeze at the pier, Sandy offered Kasey unsolicited advice. "Look, I think the way to handle this is simple," she began. "Invite him over for dinner and clear the air. You and Cadman got off on the wrong foot, and that's creating unnecessary tension. If the two of you would just hit the reset button and set the initial misunderstanding aside, I truly believe you'd find you get along nicely."

"Are you crazy?" Kasey hissed.

Sandy buttered the bun she'd taken from the basket between them. "Look, Kasey. If the man was dangerous or meant you harm, you probably would not be sitting here talking to me now."

Kasey had to consider that fact, but she asked, "Then how did he know I contacted the authorities to report his suspicious behavior?"

Her friend dismissed that with a shrug. "Maybe he doesn't know. Maybe he was fishing to see if you had seen anything? I don't know, but that's why you should get to know him better."

"You are crazy!"

Sandy smiled, shook her head. "And you mentioned you suspect he might be using drugs. I don't believe he does. You don't even know what he does for a living. For all you know, whatever you saw might have been related to his job."

"But- "

Sandy laughed. "Kasey. I honestly think you need to put your mind at ease and get to know the guy."

"But- "

"Personally, I think that whole thing with your ex has you tied up in knots, and you're projecting it onto your neighbor. Maybe you need to talk to someone."

"I'm talking to you now, aren't I?"

"As a friend, not as the amazing psychiatrist I happen to be." Sandy smiled.

Kasey sat back in her chair. Maybe Sandy was right. Perhaps she was trying to see the worst in Cadman because she hadn't looked beyond Richard's false charm. Perhaps Richard had taken away her trust of men, and Cadman was a convenient scapegoat for her because he was her neighbor.

"He would probably tell me no if I found the courage to ask him over for dinner. He'd suspect I were trying to poison him."

Sandy laughed. "And who could blame him?"

"Thanks for that."

"Come on. You can do it. You're brave. You were a nurse in Vietnam and not in a safe zone. You made it through that and didn't cower."

"I didn't have time to be afraid. The wounded kept my mind occupied."

Sandy reached out her hand, covered the top of Kasey's. "You had a breaking point, but you worked through that." She searched her friend's eyes. "You aren't having nightmares, are you?"

"No. That part of my life I could work through with no problem. That's why I can't understand why that was easy for me to let roll off my

shoulders, but I'm obsessed with finding Cadman Benson guilty of wrongdoing."

"I'm telling you. Invite him for dinner. Talk."

Kasey opened her mouth to protest, but Sandy told her, "Look. It's either try to get to know the man or find a new place to live."

Someone Like You

Chapter Ten

A week passed before Kasey found the nerve to approach Cadman and invite him to her house for dinner. She knew he would say no, but she would at least try to extend the invitation.

And there was still that matter of her wondering if he was a drug user. She would not come right out and ask him. Doing that would probably be the final nail in her coffin. But if an opportunity arose, she would broach the subject.

Walking up his sidewalk toward his front door, she rolled her eyes, thinking she probably could have come up with a better analogy than one pertaining to death when she already felt as though the man probably fantasized about killing her. If he did dream about it, she hoped it was nothing more than a metaphorical desire.

When she reached his front door, she knocked before she lost the nerve.

She heard Mutt barking, then Cadman's command for the dog to be quiet. Amazingly, the animal stopped almost immediately.

He opened the door and stared at her as though he could not comprehend she was standing there.

"Hi," she said and was proud of herself for keeping the nervousness out of her voice for a change.

He continued his scrutiny, and although she was a good five feet eight, it felt as though his six-foot frame towered over her more than before.

When he continued looking at her, saying nothing, she forced herself to continue with the reason she was standing there.

"Umm. Look, I am truly sorry for my accusations. It was wrong of me, and I was hoping we could, maybe, try to bury the hatchet and attempt to be friends."

Cadman tilted his head to one side as though studying her from a different angle. "Is this a trick?"

She held up her hands, palms out towards him. "No trick. Just honesty."

"You aren't planning of accusing me of burying a body in my backyard or something like that?"

"Well, if you do, I hope it's the sex doll you clobbered the other night."

Oh. My. God. Why would she say something like that? True, she had a sense of humor she hasn't used lately, but why it chose that moment to come out, she would never know.

He blinked. And then the most extraordinary thing happened. He smiled, and a slow chuckle rose and came out.

With a shake of his head, he told her, "You confuse the hell out of me, Kasey Evans."

"I know. And again, I am sorry. Perhaps if you come over for dinner tonight, we can clear the air between us. And if not tonight, some other time. Whatever works for you."

He ran his hands through his hair. Did he dare? Or was she going to poison him? If she honestly wanted to make amends for things in the past, then maybe he could give her a chance to half redeem herself.

"All right," he told her after letting out a long breath. "Tonight works for me. What time?"

His answer shocked her momentarily speechless. "Umm, six-thirty?"

"I'll be there," he said and shut the door.

Dazed by his answer, Kasey walked back to her house.

Thankfully, it was her day off from work. She could drive to the store and picked up ingredients for the meal she would make. After that, she cleaned her house. Not that it was a mess. She liked things tidy, but it helped take her mind off the fact Cadman Benson was coming to dinner.

* * *

She hoped he liked lasagna.

"Meow."

Glancing behind her, Kasey spotted Dolly sitting in the kitchen doorway, her big tail slowly wrapping around to cover her front legs. The cat's blue eyes seemed to be glaring at her as though she were guilty of treason.

"It is not what you think," she told the cat. "I invited the man because Sandy's right. That's what neighbors do, and I should have done it long before this."

"Meow."

"Well, yes, I think he is cute, but that has nothing to do with my asking him over. It is my way of asking for his forgiveness."

Dolly yawned.

"Now, do not act like you know different," Kasey told the big cat. "He is probably a very nice man, and if I wouldn't always jump to conclusions, we would have been friends by now."

The cat looked away.

"Well, if you're going to be like that, I might not give you a treat before bed tonight."

Dolly got up and walked away.

Kasey shook her head, knowing having this conversation with her cat was insane, but dang it, Dolly's whole demeanor tonight felt judgmental.

She was walking into the dining area with two plates and silverware in her hands when the doorbell rang.

Kasey felt her heart leap and acknowledged her nerves were a combination of things. She had never felt this way around any man, not even Richard when he was trying to win her over. Obviously, she was not looking for a relationship with Cadman Benson, as her cat seemed to imply with that look of contempt. Tonight was about two people finally getting to know each other over food and hopefully pleasant conversation. Kasey hoped they could put all the misunderstandings behind them and at least form some type of friendship.

And if Cadman had a drug problem, advice would be easier to hear from a friend than an enemy.

Setting the dishes and cutlery down on the table, she answered the door.

He looked freshly showered with his hair slicked back. He changed his clothes, and Kasey could not help but notice how nicely his crisp blue jeans formed to his body. Different from the faded ones he wore earlier. The blue T-shirt he was wearing had the logo of a cowboy and girl dancing. The words "Medora, explore it today" were printed underneath the pair of dancers.

Apparently, he collected t-shirts that advertised that particular place, and she wondered where it was located.

"Hi," he said. "Am I early?"

"Not at all. I was just setting the table. I hope you like lasagna, it will be ready in five minutes. I just need to put some garlic toast in to heat up." She turned away before she did something stupid and salivate. Cadman was very pleasing on the eyes.

"Make yourself at home." She gestured toward the living room. "Feel free to turn on the television."

He shrugged. "Na. The only thing that comes on tonight I'd want to watch is Starsky and Hutch."

She stopped arranging the table for a moment and exclaimed, "I love Starsky and Hutch!"

He moved towards the table, pulled out a chair and sat down. "Really? I had you figured as a Mary Tyler Moore fan."

Shaking her head as she laughed, "Mary Tyler Moore is funny, but I'm more of an action type person."

He almost laughed. The fact Kasey liked police drama might be why she was always looking for trouble.

She continued with placing the silverware and elaborated upon her love of police shows. "Gravitating toward those types of entertainment is probably why I volunteered to go to Vietnam. And believe me. That should have been enough action to last me a lifetime, but I am a sucker for police dramas."

Cadman blinked. "You were in Nam?" He was shocked.

"As a nurse with the Red Cross. Before that, I was in Korea." She shuddered. "I always had the desire to serve my country, and I figured what better way to do that than to be there and help save the lives of our soldiers."

Her revelation astonished him. Red Cross nurses were a special breed, traveling to unknown destinations and helping people in need. It took guts to volunteer for duty in Vietnam. Nurses faced an endless influx of casualties, and wounded soldiers brought in daily. The living conditions were harsh, and there was always the real possibility of being shot or killed.

Kasey had no way of knowing she earned his respect because of that, despite his dislike of her since the first time they met. Perhaps there were reasons she was always suspicious. It did not excuse her behavior toward him, but he could understand it.

She met his gaze briefly before saying, "I'll bring out the lasagna." And with that, she walked back to the kitchen. When she returned, he asked, "What are you doing working in a hardware store? Or do you also work at a hospital too?"

Handing him the plated lasagna, she told him, "I retired from nursing recently. My dad owns the hardware store, and when he asked me to come back to town to help him, I said yes. Besides, I was ready for a change in my life. After I returned from Nam, I went to work as a trauma nurse at a hospital in LA. A combination of things had me wanting to leave the profession and come home." She shrugged, "I grew up here, and I needed a break from the blood and gore."

She shook her head. "I am sorry, that is not exactly dinner conversation." She plated her own stacked layers of pasta before sitting down across from him.

He understood her desire for change more than she knew. There were things he'd seen over the year's most people could not stomach. Bodies torn apart from a grenade, men bleeding out from gunshot wounds, not to mention witnessing acts by others beyond comprehension.

Humans did horrific things to their fellow man. There would always be someone in the sandbox who wanted to be king and would do everything in their power to get there.

"It's all right," he told her. "Sometimes a person has to talk about it before it gets bottled up inside. The mind can only handle so much before it needs a release from the images it holds." He knew firsthand what it was like to sometimes want to give up hope, but he was fortunate enough to have his best friend Colten Fisher to talk to when things got to him.

And there was always the task force psychiatrist who loved to evaluate a person to death. Cadman avoided the woman like the plague. He did not believe in letting some damn shrink play with his head, especially

one who had never seen combat. The doctor would piss her pants if she ever experienced some of the missions he had been on.

Kasey tried not to stare at him. He seemed to grasp exactly what she struggled to explain to those who felt the need to berate her for leaving her nursing career. People never took the time to ask why she needed to step away; they only wanted to offer their opinion. After transitioning directly from the Vietnam War into intense trauma work back in the States, her mind desperately needed time away. Caring for soldiers with little chance of survival was profoundly stressful; she would sit with them for hours, knowing all she could offer was a glimmer of hope in a hopeless situation. The trauma unit back home was no less intense, a constant barrage of car accidents, shootings, and drug overdoses. After years of experiencing so much, she needed space to reflect and find what made her happy again. She had sacrificed for others, and now she needed time for herself.

And now that she had established her credentials, she commented, "I think the worst things I saw during my time in L.A. were the junkies. I've seen many people go from healthy, successful people to become shells of their former self." She reached for a slice of garlic toast, put it on her place as she casually asked, "Have you known anyone with a drug problem?"

Cadman shook his head. "I've been fortunate enough not to have a friend or loved one succumb to their power, but I've seen the effects it has on people who use. I know the government tries to stop the infestation of them coming into the country. It's a major problem. One that is hard to control because the cartel is organized. Their drug trafficking operations are hard to shut down."

Well, that had not caused him to admit he had a problem, but he seemed to understand how the system of illegal drugs coming into the country worked.

Not knowing what else to say on the subject, she took a bite of the pasta, amazed it tasted good. Having not cooked often, she was afraid

the meal would be tasteless. She did not want the man sitting on the opposite side of the table to have something else to dislike her for.

"This is fantastic," he told her. "And a hell of a lot better than my mother's. You hid the flavor of the poison very well."

Kasey stared at him, then burst out laughing. "Thanks. It's a special talent of mine, but I doubt it's better than your mom's but thank you for the compliment."

He could not prevent himself from smiling at her. He had not meant to tease her, yet she had taken it in stride. And as to his mother's cooking, he was being honest. His mother was not the best cook in the world.

"So, may I ask what you do for a living?" she said.

He had thought about what to tell her, knowing the question would probably come up at some point tonight. He could not tell her the truth, but he did not want to lie to her either.

The best strategy was to sick with the standard line he told his friends and family. Consistency was key, and he would not get trapped by a lie. "I'm in the Secret Service." Not really a lie. His work was secret, and it was a service to the American people, even if they did not know about it.

"Really?" her eyes widened. Oh, god. If that were true, it would explain so much! Maybe he had not been buying drugs that day when she saw him in the alley talking to the homeless man. Or perhaps the man was undercover and reporting to him?

Kasey mentally shook herself and knew she should probably stop reading spy novels, as much as she loved them. They filled her head with too many scenarios.

She was about to ask him what it was like to be a Secret Service agent when she noticed his fork seemed frozen at his lips. His eyes were staring at something over her shoulder.

Turning, she saw Dolly sitting in the kitchen doorway, staring back at Cadman.

"What," Cadman whispered, "in the hell is that?"

Kasey almost laughed. His reaction was typical of someone who had never seen Dolly before.

A four-foot-long, twenty-eight-pound feline was unusual, and especially because Dolly was a female, and they generally were smaller.

"She's my cat."

He shook his head. "That's not a cat. It's the size of a beagle."

Laughing and enjoying the comparison, she told him, "Dolly is a Maine Coon."

Now Cadman's eyes slowly moved off the cat to look at Kasey. "A what?"

"A Maine Coon. They are the largest breed of domestic cats."

Kasey called to the feline. "Come on, Dolly… come here. It is all right. Come and meet Cadman."

Cadman shook his head. "The thing is fine where it's at."

She raised a brow. "You dislike cats?"

"Cats are fine, but that cannot be a one."

With a laugh, she reached out and called to her pet once more. "Come on, Dolly Pawdon. I will give you a treat if you do."

His chuckle started slow. "You named your cat Dolly Pawdon?"

"Sure. Why not? Look how beautiful she is. I thought she looked like one of Dolly Parton's big wigs, all white, big and fluffy. And besides, look who is talking. You named your dog, Mutt."

His laughter was heightened with that statement. Kasey earned a point with that one. It surprised him to realize he liked Kasey Evans, regardless of her suspicious nature. She obviously had a good sense of humor, though he had not seen a lot of it up until now, and she understood the horrors of war.

The telephone in her living room rang. She excused herself to answer it.

Cadman went back to eating his meal; watchful of that thing she called a cat. He had never seen a house cat of that size, and it fascinated him.

"Damn it, Richard! Please stop calling me! This harassment needs to end."

Turning in his chair, Cadman watched Kasey slam the receiver back into its cradle. It was none of his business, but that did not prevent him from asking, "What was that about?"

The mood turned serious as Kasey walked back to the table to sit down. "My ex-husband," she explained. "We have been divorced for almost seven months, but Richard doesn't seem to get that fact. He calls me repeatedly to inform me he thought I made a mistake divorcing him and that I have to come back because I need him." She pushed her half-eaten plate of lasagna away from her, no longer hungry.

The fact she'd been married did not surprise him. Any man that was lucky enough to gain her love and lose it, Cadman could only assume, was a dumbass. Although why he suddenly felt that way, when not more than seven hours ago, he had wanted to drop kick her to the moon, he could not say.

"So is Dick dangerous?" It was natural for his mind to be suspicious. In his line of work, he was always on full alert and men who hassled women were nothing short of bullies and sometimes dangerous ones at that.

"Richard?" She shook her head. "I did not divorce him because he was physically abusive. After six months of marriage, I was done with him and his overblown opinion of himself. He believed all the household chores were my responsibility. It did not concern him in the least that I

put in way more hours than he did at the hospital. His ego is the size of Montana, and he believes he must have the best of everything. He is a doctor in L.A. and granted, he is very good at what he does, but if you listen to him long enough, he will have you believing he is the best there is anywhere in the world."

"How in the world did you wind up marrying the guy?"

She threw her hands in the air. "I have asked myself that same question countless times. I do not know how I let myself get sucked in by his lies. Everything he did was calculated and subtle. When I first met him, he was charming and captivating. He pretended to find everything I valued as important and interesting. He wanted to do everything I did, saying those were his interests too."

Cadman was seeing why she was a suspicious person.

She shrugged. "He made me feel cherished, valued, and significant. Looking back now, I don't understand how he manipulated my feelings. I never was the type of person to feel inadequate about myself. Little by little, he got me to believe he was the greatest thing to have ever happen to me."

She made a face, still boggled by the fact she'd fallen for the lunatic.

"Everything changed once you married him?" Cadman asked, figuring it did not take the dick long to show his true colors.

She shook her head. "You have that right. Once we were married, he did a one-eighty. Suddenly what I wanted was stupid, and it was all about him."

"Did he abuse you physically?" He wanted to be clear on that issue because he had the urge to track the man down and scare the living shit out of him.

She wrinkled her nose. "Richard? No. Not physically. Verbally, yes! Especially after I told him I wanted a divorce. I am not afraid of him. I

just want him to stop calling me and move on with his life. I certainly have."

"The next time he calls, and he will, tell him you are reporting his harassment to the police. Which you should do if you haven't already done so."

"I doubt the police will care that my ex-husband is begging me to come back to him." They had not given a fig about her reporting her neighbor of suspicious behavior. The same neighbor who was now in her house, and she was enjoying their time together.

She regretted her quick judgments of him.

"If they don't, let me know. I'll make damn sure they understand that ignoring this guy is not an option." He took another bite of the pasta and motioned with his fork towards the direction of the telephone. He added, "Better yet, change your phone number too."

"I requested a new number with the phone company just the other day."

"Good, but you should still call the police and report him, or I can do it for you."

Kasey stared at him, and she wondered if he was much more than a Secret Service agent. The Secret Service did not have any authority over local law enforcement. Yet, Cadman seemed convinced all he needed to do was have a conversation with them, and they would listen to him. And there was that little fact he seemed to know she had reported him to the authorities.

She knew she was doing it again, assuming things. But she could not help thinking either Cadman was not Secret Service, or he was something else entirely.

Chapter Eleven

When the meal was over, Cadman was not as eager as he had thought he would have been to head back home. He did not like uncomfortable small talk or awkward silence, so he had planned his exit strategy in advance for when the time came. Being prepared was something he prided himself on.

However, Kasey intrigued him. Despite how they met, his first impression of her, and the last few weeks, he was slowly seeing her from a different perspective.

Kasey was really a fascinating person. She shared a few stories from her time in Vietnam. She told him how, at her request, the Red Cross agreed to assign her to an evacuation hospital in the rural district of Ho Chi Minh City. She had heard that there was a tremendous need for nurses at that location. She was quick on her feet and knew what a doctor needed before they asked. She knew her skills had the potential to save more lives if she went to a front-line hospital. Cadman's admiration for her grew with each story she told. The Base Camp there had been one of the most active locations.

His desire to share his own horrifying experiences with her was astounding; such confessions had always been reserved solely for Colton. While he wanted to convey his deep understanding of the pain she carried, he recognized the absolute impossibility of it. Any personal detail would inevitably lead to questions; like why a Secret Service agent was in the jungles of South America. Questions that would instantly compromise his cover if he were to answer them.

Instead, he remained silent and listened to her accounts. He understood the depths of her emotions. She had no way of knowing the empathy and respect he had for her. He had spent years deliberately learning to numb his mind, forcing himself not to dwell on the horrific scenes: the

blood, the shattered bodies, and the loss of arms, legs, and eyes when the "bad guys" fought back. He had witnessed the ultimate personal suffering inflicted by those consumed with a need to control and conquer, showing no regard for humanity.

Kasey's vivid descriptions instantly made him think of the men he lost during his career with the Task Force. He shoved the feelings and memories aside, refusing to let them take hold. While he would never forget his fallen comrades, he knew the pain would compromise his focus, making it impossible for him to execute his duties efficiently.

He could not even tell her he had been in Vietnam himself a time or two when Task Force Ghost was in its infancy, and the United States needed to increase their military forces in South Vietnam. His team had helped in the hot spots, coming in behind the Viet Cong when and where they could. Sometimes they saved some villagers who had been living peacefully until their village became the middle of the battleground.

Sometimes, his team was not so lucky, and they lost lives.

And that was the pain of war he had a tough time forgetting. Also, the incredible heat over there, and the stench of death. It took a long time to leave the nostrils once you left the country, and the mission was over.

He helped her wash the dishes after dinner was through, and they moved into the living room.

“How long were in Nam?” he asked as they sat on her couch.

"I was there from sixty-five to seventy-two," she said. "I'd meant to stay longer, but one day..." She shook her head, paused for a cleansing breath. "I just knew I'd had enough of the bloodshed. I couldn't block the horrors out anymore, and I had to leave."

Cadman wanted to reach out, take her hand in his.

“What happened?” Why he asked, he was not sure, but something within himself wanted to know what became her breaking point.

She remained silent for a beat, making Cadman think she was done, before she whispered, "They brought a little boy into the O.R. tent. He was hit by artillery; his village was under fire just for being in a battle zone. His lower body was severely burned, and he was losing blood fast." The surgeons worked for hours to save him. Once they were through, Kasey helped move the child to a corner of the hospital tent, and she collapsed. She'd assisted in countless operations on children in Vietnam, but seeing that poor boy, knowing he would never walk again, she realized her capacity to cope was gone. She could no longer numb the pain.

Kasey swiped away the tears for that little boy and took in a deep breath. "My service to the Red Cross was up anyway, and I needed to come home."

He swallowed a lump in his throat. He had witnessed countless children being slaughtered by the Viet Cong during his missions to Vietnam. And even recently when his team had gone into a remote area of El Salvador. His team was not always able to save everyone.

She took another cleansing breath. "When I got back stateside, I thought I'd had enough with trauma. But while I stayed with friends in California, I became restless. I took a job at the hospital in the emergency room. I was so used to a fast pace, it seemed natural for me to apply." She shrugged. "But after my marriage to Richard soured, and constantly dealing with suffering, I needed a change." Kasey shook her head. "I am here now, helping my parents and enjoying the low stress." She chuckled. "The worst that happens at the store is if someone drops a hammer on their foot, and I can deal with that easily enough."

"Do you miss being a nurse?"

Cocking her head to the side, she considered the question for a moment. "Actually, not as much as I would have thought after having been one for years."

She smiled. "And what about you, Mr. Benson? Obviously, the Secret Service keeps you busy. When I first moved into the neighborhood, you were never home. At least, I only saw Mutt and Becky, and we will not talk about that, okay? I hope you'll forgive me for my assumptions about your relationship with her."

He laughed. "It was kind of flattering in a way. The fact you would think a teenager would go for a forty-nine-year-old."

"You look really good for your age." Her face flushed, realizing what she said and was thankful she had not told him he was mouthwatering gorgeous.

Thankfully, he did not get offended. "Well, I do not know how old you are, and I won't ask, but you look good too."

"I'm forty-five."

She looked younger, but as much as he wanted to tell her she was a beautiful woman, he would tread lightly. One never knew how a woman would react when discussing their age.

Kasey was gallant enough to change the subject back to his absenteeism when she first moved into the neighborhood. "So," she prompted, "your job keeps you away from home a lot?"

"Actually, most weeks, I am home more often than not. There were a few things that needed my attention, but now, unless something dire comes up, you'll probably tire of seeing my mug around."

Kasey somehow doubted that but would not consider why that could be.

She stood up, crossed to the television. "How about watching an episode of Black Sheep Squadron with me?"

He could not believe she wanted to watch his favorite military drama, but it should not have surprised him when she had confessed to liking fast action television dramas. "You know what, yeah. That sounds good," and was surprised how much the idea of watching an episode with her appealed to him.

Oh, my hell. Cadman thought about what his mother said about needing someone in his life because he was lonely. There was no way his mother could be right. He was not looking for a relationship with anyone, and besides, if he were, he could just hear his mother gloating in her singsong I told you so speech.

God knew he had heard enough of those to last a lifetime.

Together they watched Black Sheep Squadron, not caring it was a rerun of the one that aired in February. At 8:00 pm, they watched the medical action-adventure show, Emergency!

At 9:00 pm, Cadman told her goodnight and headed home.

He walked the short distance across her lawn to his yard, but thoughts of Kasey followed him through the front door.

There was something about Kasey Evans that drew him to her in ways he was not sure he liked.

Perhaps it was the shock of discovering she had been in Nam and could understand his life had his heart twisted up.

But he knew one damn thing. He never had, nor ever would, moon over a woman.

Chapter Twelve

As the days passed, Kasey and Cadman reached a point where they were no longer at each other's throats but were on friendly terms. There were a few times when Kasey came home with a few bags of groceries cradled in her arms and Cadman would offer to help carry them into the house for her. Which was an offer she would never refuse. Groceries sometimes could be a bit heavy, especially when she'd picked up a hundred-pound bag of Dolly's kibble.

They'd also gotten together at Kasey's house one night to watch Conspiracy of Terror on her television. They munched on popcorn and drank a few beers as they watched the 1975 comedy-drama. The story was about a husband-and-wife detective team who investigate a case of a man who literally was scared to death.

On other days they would not see each other at all, which Kasey was glad for because she was developing feelings for her neighbor that were not neighborly.

A few months after her first dinner night with Cadman she arranged another lunch date with her friend Sandy, who appeared to be eager to hear how things had gone that night, and perhaps discover if there was any budding romance in that department.

Kasey had to laugh over that. Sandy sure seemed hell bent on placing Cadman on the boyfriend list.

"He's actually a nice man," Kasey told her as they sat at a table at the same restaurant they'd gone to down by the pier the last time they'd gotten together and had discussed the same person they were now. "And I think he's forgiven me for my blunders."

Sandy used her folk to point at her. "I told you. All you needed to do was get to know him. I knew he would complement you nicely." She

paused. "Let me rephrase that. I didn't mean that as it sounded. I meant I hoped the two of you would get along so you wouldn't have to move."

Kasey narrowed her eyes. "That almost sounds like you know him. Is there something you aren't telling me?"

"Don't be ridiculous. How could I possibly know your neighbor? I was basing my assumption of our conversation a few weeks ago."

"Umm."

Sandy shrugged. "Believe what you want." She glanced at her watch. "I've got about fifteen more minutes before I need to go back to work."

When the time was up, they parted ways, and Kasey tried not to turn her suspicions on her friend.

When Kasey arrived at work, she grabbed a box of products that needed to be stocked and got to work, putting them on the shelf.

"Hey, Kas-adilla."

At the familiar nickname, Kasey looked up from her task of stocking a shelf and smiled at her father.

"Hey, back, Daddy-O."

Ed Davis was a spry sixty-five-year-old who showed no sign of slowing down. Kasey believed it was because he had a strong work ethic and did not enjoy sitting around doing nothing.

Both of her parents were hard workers. Her mother, Claris, would help at the store now and again when there was an unexpected need. She was more than happy to fill in when an employee called in sick or did not show up for a shift. Over the years, there were times when employees could not or were not willing to work a few extra hours to help cover a shift. Claris Davis would put aside whatever she was doing and come in to cover the hours.

There was nothing worse than an employee who constantly grumbled about not having enough money but had no issue taking a personal day

off without pay. Her parents always said money did not grow on trees. If someone wanted to be successful in life, they needed to do what it took to reach that goal.

Ed stopped in front of his youngest daughter and smiled. “How are things going at your place?”

Kasey stood up and brushed at her pants leg to remove dirt gathered there from her kneeling on the floor. “Actually, the kitchen sink sprung a leak this morning. Malcolm is going to come over later tonight and fix it.”

“That’s nice of him.”

She smiled. “It sure is nice having a plumber for a brother.”

Ed nodded. “The boy makes me proud.” He reached down into the box of Firestarter Kasey had been stocking and placed a few of the items on the shelf.

“Mom and I want to thank you again for helping us out. It’s greatly appreciated.” He cleared his throat, and Kasey knew he was about to say something he was not comfortable with but would say it anyway.

“Mother and I are delighted to have you back home with us, you know. All those years you were in Vietnam kept us worried.”

Kasey gave him a quick hug. “I know, and I am sorry for the stress it caused you both. I think it helped tame my ambitions to help on the battlefield.”

Ed grinned. “Good. I am also sorry your marriage to Richard did not work out, but since it didn’t, I won’t mind telling you I didn’t like the little weasel.”

She put her hand on her hip. “You couldn’t have told me that before I married the jerk?”

“You know you wouldn’t have listened to me and would have married him anyway.”

He was probably right. She had always been headstrong.

"Anyway," her father continued, "How is Dolly doing?"

"She's great, and you know you and mom are welcome to visit her at any time." Kasey glanced over her father's shoulder, feeling her heart skip a beat when she saw Cadman Benson standing near the paint, browsing the color choices.

Her father noticed his daughter's distraction and looked over his shoulder too. What he saw was a potential paying customer, not the sparkle that, until now, had been missing in his daughter's eye.

Ed turned and was about to head in the man's direction to make a sale but Kasey reached out, touched her father's arm and said, "I will help him."

Her father's brow cocked upward as he watched his daughter walk past him. Kasey hated the painting section. She always avoided the aisle as though a plague lived there. They even made a deal before she began working at the store. His daughter let him know that on the days he was working, the painting department was his domain, and she would do everything else.

He shrugged and continued stocking the shelves his daughter had been working on when he interrupted her. If she wanted to suddenly become a paint expert, he would let her. Besides, the man she was talking to did not look like a shmuck. Perhaps his daughter would find him foxy, as the kids liked to say. He hoped his daughter was ready to date again. The good Lord knew she deserved to have someone in her life to keep her company during the night.

Ed blushed at the thought. He could not believe he just wished his daughter had a man to share a bed with. Shaking the idea out of his head, he bent down to stock the lower shelves.

Kasey walked up to Cadman. "Hi," she smiled.

Cadman glanced up from the row of paint swatches; grinned. "Hi, back." He grabbed a paint sample called Osage Orange and frowned.

Kasey could not help but laugh at the face he was making. "If you dislike orange so much, why would you pick it?"

He put the sample back as he shook his head. "It isn't for me. I promised my mother I would paint her living room this weekend. She decided orange would spice up the room. I think it is ridiculous."

Kasey now understood his predicament. "Well, umm… it is an interesting color choice."

He grabbed another swatch but put it back. "Mom's a bit weird."

She shook her head, laughed. "Cadman!" she exclaimed.

Cadman looked at Kasey, chuckled. "Only the truth. Want to guess what color her bathroom is?"

"Green?"

"Flamingo pink with purple trim."

She bit her bottom lip, trying not to laugh harder than she had already. "Oh, my."

Taking a step back from the samples, Cadman motioned to them and said, "Help me out here, Kasey. What would you pick?"

"Not orange," she told him as she moved forward to look over the swatches.

"She will have my head if it's anything other than orange."

Kasey giggled at the thought of this muscular man being afraid of his mother. "Did she say how dark or light this mandated orange had to be?"

"Nope! Just orange."

Reaching out, Kasey grabbed two color samples. "Here, show these to her. You could use this orange color on the wall that would be the main

focal point of the room. Then use this harvest yellow color on the three other walls. That way, your mom gets the pop of orange color that she wants but this shade will ease your anti-orange frustration when you are sitting in the room."

Intrigued, Cadman looked at her. He never thought of using more than one color to paint a room.

"Does she have a rug?"

"Are you talking about in the living room?"

She nodded.

"Nope. Plan hardwood."

"Then I have another suggestion to go with the paint. Let me show you."

She led him across the store where the area rugs were on display. Pointing, she said, "Get her this one." The large shag rug contained a rich dark brown crisscrossed through a maze of colors similar to the color swatches she gave him in the paint aisle.

"After the painting is done, you lay this on the floor, and I bet she will be thrilled with the whole thing."

He stared at her. "Are you sure you were a nurse? Because you are a hell of a salesman. I'll take it all and blame you if my mom doesn't like it."

Smiling, she told him, "I bet she will love it."

This time when he grinned, she could see the dimple on his cheek, which made her feel a quick flutter of sensation in her stomach.

"So now we have a bet going on?" he said.

"I did not…" She stopped herself, and playfully said, "I guess we do."

"Ok, then you're on. What's the wager going to be?"

She chuckled, "You tell me, you are the one turning this into a game."

Cadman put a hand to his beard, stroking his chin between his thumb and fingers as he considered the terms of the bet. “How about this, if my mom hates it, you owe me a cup of coffee? If she loves it, I buy.”

She shook her head, still grinning. “What kind of bet is that?”

“A cheap one, because I know my mom. She will hate the whole thing, and I don’t want to take advantage of you for not knowing the woman.”

“Gee, I appreciate your concern.”

“You’re welcome. Now mix me up some of that paint, while I figure out how to stuff that rug into my Firebird.”

“You don’t want to show her the samples first?”

“Nope. She told me to pick up the paint, which is her way of blaming me if the color is wrong.”

“Umm.” She had no words for that. It did not seem fair to expect someone else to choose paint colors without approving them first.

Cadman looked around for a few brushes and rollers while Kasey mixed the paint.

“These are ready to go,” she said as she put the cans of mixed paint on the counter. “If you are ready, I can help you carry them to the checkout.”

“Are you sure you don’t want to frisk me first?” Cadman said with a devious smile. Kasey felt a flush of heat rush to her face as it covered her face with embarrassment. She looked up at him sheepishly and began to say, “You do have the right to remain silent….”

Suddenly they heard a female voice shriek, “Oh my, God! Cadman Benson, is that you?”

Cadman turned around to see the person belonging to the voice. At first, he was not sure if he recognized the woman. She was vaguely familiar, but he could not quite place her.

The woman laughed. “Brenda Davis,” she held out her hand to greet him, “Well, it hasn’t been Davis for about thirty years, but in high school, it was Davis.”

Unexpectedly she began clapping her hands in rhythm and started shouting, “Cadman… Cadman, he’s our man!” clap, clap, clap. “Cadman… has a plan!” clap, clap, clap. “You can’t win! We’ve got Cadman in command!”

“B.D.!” Cadman exclaimed, shaking his head with the memories the cheer conjured up from his days on the high school football team. “God, that cheer feels like a lifetime ago.”

He turned toward Kasey as he said, “Hey, this is Brenda…”

“Nord,” Kasey finished. “Yes, I know.” She looked at the woman and said, “Hey, Sis. How’s your day going?”

Chapter Thirteen

Kasey was struck by a ridiculous jealousy the instant she learned her sister and Cadman had known each other in high school and why had she never met him when her sister was a cheerleader back then?

Because she'd been fourteen at the time and had not cared about football jocks or stupid cheers, that's why.

Brenda chatted with Cadman while Kasey tried her best to not make faces at her sibling for bursting in out of nowhere and interrupting.

"Maybe you could come over for supper some night? Brett would love to see you!"

"So, you and Brett got hitched, eh? What's he up to nowadays?"

"He's an electrician now. We own Nord Electric. If you are ever in need of an electrician, give us a call."

"I'll do that," Cadman said.

Brenda babbled some more. At least it sounded like babbling to Kasey's ears. It seemed as though her sister would not shut up anytime soon.

"Hey Kasey," Brenda suddenly said, turning her attention away from Cadman. "Malcolm mentioned he was going to stop by your house tonight and fix a leaky faucet in your kitchen."

Cadman's ears perked up. "You have a leak?" he asked. "I can fix it for you." And whoever this Malcolm was could stay away from Kasey.

Now, why on earth was he upset about some unknown man fixing something for Kasey?

"Really?" Kasey asked. "That would be great. I can tell my brother he does not have to drive out of his way after work tonight."

Brenda's ears went on alert. "You two know each other?"

"We're neighbors," they said in unison.

This time it was Brenda's turn to say, "Really?" Cadman wondered if Brenda had taken lessons from his mother on how to make one-word sound so over-exaggerated.

"Yes, really," Kasey told her sister. "Don't you have something to do?"

"Not particularly," Brenda said. "Besides, I stopped by to see dad and to ask you how you're doing. Is Richard still pestering you?"

"Changing my phone number helped," Kasey wished she never had to hear that name again. "It has been peaceful lately."

The pager on Cadman's hip buzzed. He scowled when he read the message.

"Sorry, I have to go." He pulled out his wallet, "Is it possible to hold the rug here? I can take the paint with me, but I don't have time to struggle with the rug right now."

Kasey rang up the sale and told him, "How about I bring everything home with me? You can pick it up tonight when you come over to fix the faucet?"

"You wouldn't mind?" Cadman asked.

"Not at all."

"That would be fantastic, and I appreciate it."

Cadman tossed some money on the counter to cover the cost of the paint and rug. "Thanks, Kasey, see you later."

Both women watched him walk away.

Once Cadman was out of earshot, Brenda turned toward Kasey and wiggled her brows. "You lucky girl."

"What do you mean by that?"

Laughing, Brenda told her, "Oh, come on! You live next door to Cadman Benson!" She gave a dreamy sigh. "I've always had a crush on that man.

Kasey did not want to hear about her sister's crush. "You're married."

"So?"

"So, you shouldn't be crushing on someone other than your husband."

"Oh, please. There is no way you can tell me you don't think he's attractive. Those biceps of his make my mouth water. I wish Brett had arms like that."

Kasey was not about to discuss with her sister how attractive she found Cadman, so she said nothing at all.

Brenda was three years older, and they had never been close. Brenda married young. At eighteen, she and Brett decided to elope and moved out of the family home, much to their parents' dismay. Three years later, when Kasey reached the age of eighteen, she also left home to attend nursing school and joined the Red Cross. Occasionally they corresponded through letters, but those had been far and few in-between through the years.

Both siblings had separate lives, and neither of them were looking to become best friends.

"Did you need something, Brenda?" Kasey asked.

"No. I'll just say hi to daddy before heading home. Is he in the backroom?"

Kasey glanced around, looking for their father. "Maybe… or in his office."

Brenda turned to head toward the manager's office but paused for a moment, looking back at her sister she said, "Kasey, I know Richard was a jerk, and I will not judge you for that huge mistake you made in marrying the guy."

No, but you sure as hell had to get that little dig in, Kasey thought.

"And I truly stopped by to ask if Richard was still bothering you. I'm glad he's not. Also, I want you to know…" she hesitated. "Cadman is a very nice man. I'm just surprised someone hasn't snatched him up by now."

Kasey watched her sister walk away and could not help wondering what, exactly, was Brenda implying?

With a sigh, Kasey gathered the paint and put the paint cans in a shopping cart before heading to grab the rug. She would store the items in the office until it was time for her to clock out, then she would take them home with her.

She had no idea she was humming a happy tune as her mind drifted. She was looking forward to Cadman coming over tonight. Even though she would never admit it out loud, she agreed with Brenda.

Cadman's biceps were mouthwatering.

* * *

Cadman climbed into his Firebird, headed to the Whitehouse. As he drove, he could not believe how territorial he felt when he thought an other man would be at Kasey's house tonight. Seriously, he thought to himself. What was he thinking? Malcolm was her brother for god's sake. Not that he knew it at the time when he quickly offered Kasey help, but seriously, what had gotten into him?

He switched lanes; glad he rolled down the windows to let air circulate. He chastised himself for his quick response to Kasey's need. "I'll fix your leak!" He blurted out loud as he stopped at a red light. The man stopped in the car next to him, glanced in his direction with a look of horror.

Cadman shifted in his seat as he realized what he shouted, and the sexual implication of the phrase. Shit. He might as well be a cat marking

his territory. He was not the jealous type or a man to expect an exclusive relationship with a woman.

Even when he had been Rosalinda's lover, he was never foolish enough to believe she hadn't taken others to her bed. Nor had he been resentful of that fact. But tonight, when the thought of another man showing interest in Kasey took hold, he had become possessive.

Cadman glanced at himself in the rearview mirror. "Idiot," he told himself. He had been forcing himself to stay away from her. Ever since she cooked him dinner, and he learned her story, she filled his thoughts day and night.

Damn her.

When he would take Mutt for a run, he would secretly hope for a glimpse of her, which was ridiculous. And he would carry her groceries into her house like a lovesick puppy.

For the love of Christ! He had been the one to suggest they have a movie night together. Worst of all, he enjoyed her company so much he was looking forward to doing it again.

Maybe he was having thoughts of her because he had not had sex for a while. Perhaps he should call up one of the women he knew who only wanted sex and gladly left in the morning with no strings attached.

But even as the thought occurred, it disappeared just as quickly.

None of those women seemed to appeal to him now.

"Shake it off," he told himself, as he slowed down and turned toward the gates of the Whitehouse, stopping for the real Secret Service guys to check his ID. Even though they knew him, no one took anything for granted when it came to be protecting the President of the United States.

When Cadman wove his way to the oval office, he found President Ford sitting behind his desk talking to head officials from a counter-terrorism division. Cadman would have to wait at the door.

He hated waiting, but it was a necessary part of the job. As far as the officials speaking with the president knew, he was of no importance.

Sigh. Why did he continue to do this job when only a handful of people knew what he did for America?

Because he loved his country, that was why. As long as he breathed and was healthy, he would do whatever it took to keep the borders safe. Even if that meant not being acknowledged as an asset to his country. Or his mother receiving a medal in his honor, if a time would come that his work cost him his life.

The meeting Ford was having lasted for a half-hour. As the officials were leaving, the President motioned Cadman into a room adjacent to the Oval office.

When the door closed, Ford said, "I need to send you to Libya. There seems to be a situation going on that requires your team."

Chapter Fourteen

Kasey looked at the dripping faucet, then glanced at the clock on the wall.

9:32 p.m.

Seriously? Malcolm would have been here and gone by now had she not agreed to Cadman's offer to fix the leak.

"Do you think he forgot?" Kasey asked Dolly.

She really needed to stop talking to her cat.

It was too late tonight to call her brother and ask him to come over.

He would, and rightly so, curse a blue streak if she were to do such a thing.

Sigh.

"Come on, Dolly. We will find a good book to read for an hour before calling it a night."

Kasey had just reached for the book titled Plagues and Peoples, a book on epidemiological history, by William H. McNeill, having decided to stop reading spy novels for a while, when her doorbell rang.

"Finally," she whispered under her breath.

When she opened the door, she tried hard not to show her annoyance with his late arrival.

"Kasey," Cadman said, once the door opened a crack. "I am so, so sorry! I got called into a meeting, and I could not get away from it. I would have called, but there wasn't an opportunity to do so."

"Hmm," was all she said.

Cadman's facial expression showed remorse before bowing his head in shame. "I deserve that, I suppose." Testing the waters of her temper or forgiveness, he held up his tool belt. "Do you still need that leak fixed?"

She could not seem to stay mad at him. He looked so apologetic, like a little boy who had done something wrong. His pitiful look pulled at her heart.

With her right hand, she motioned him in. "It's the kitchen faucet," she reminded him as he followed behind her. "I guess I should be grateful you came over this late." She shook her head. "That came out wrong. I am thankful."

Cadman examined the top of the faucet by turning the water on, then off again. Squatting down, he opened the cupboard below, reaching in to turn off the water supply. "I think it might need a new washer."

"Well, swell, I do not have one of those, and it's too late to get one…."

Cadman dug into his pants pocket and pulled an assortment of washers out. "I do! I always have a few on hand and put a few in my pocket before I came over thinking, hoping, this was all it needed. I believe this will fit." He held one up for her to see.

"My hero," Kasey giggled, finding humor in the fact he had what she needed.

He grinned.

"This won't take long," he told her and set to work unscrewing handle knobs.

True to his word, less than ten minutes later, her faucet was in working condition and not a drip in sight.

"Thank you," she told him. "What do I owe you?"

Oh, boy. The number of things he wanted to ask for as payment flipped through his mind, but he was not that type of guy, so said instead, "Not

a thing. You already pre-paid when you brought my paint and rug home with you."

"They are still in my car. Can I help you take them to your house?"

He shook his head. "I can manage." He hooked the tool belt to his waist so his hands could be free to carry the rug and paint.

She walked him to the front door. Opening the door, she noticed a black van backing out of his driveway. She frowned to herself as she read the words Doggy Kennel and Spa on its side and realized it was the same van that came to the house several times before to care for his dog. "Where's Mutt going?"

Cadman watched as the van drove down the block, turning out of sight.

He felt bad for having to send Mutt to doggy care, but he was not sure how long he would be in Libya.

"He's off to visit friends," Cadman said. "He does that sometimes."

"Does that mean you're leaving?" She had not meant to sound disappointed, but she was. It had been months before she learned he was her neighbor, and just as they were becoming friends, he was disappearing.

"It's job-related, and one reason I was late getting here." As he stood there looking at her, he felt a strong urge to kiss her goodbye and found himself wanting to tell her where he was going, and why. But he knew he could not. He had known no one that made him feel the way she did. And with certainty, no one ever hijacked his every thought as she seemed to do.

Maybe it was a good thing he was leaving for a while. If he were lucky, he could get her out of his head while he was gone. He knew his mission weighed heavily on him being able to do just that.

Locating bombs required a person without distractions.

Disarming them when found demanded one's undivided attention.

Nothing could ruin your day worse than suddenly finding yourself no longer in this world. And your dearly departed grandma was hovering over you announcing you too were dead.

"Oh," Kasey frowned. "Then, I wish you safe travels, and I'll hope your mother isn't too disappointed that her living room won't get painted this weekend."

He shrugged. "It isn't the first time I've had to break a promise to her. But I talked my brother Finn into doing my dirty work. He and his wife agreed to take care of the painting. Besides, they can deal with mom's complaints if she does not like the paint I…. I mean you, picked out." He chuckled.

Cadman loved his mother. He really did. He just wished the woman were not so, so, so…. He could not think of the term.

Intense? Fickle? Strange?

Ha! You decide. Whichever word you chose, you would not be wrong.

"That was nice of you," Kasey told him, and appreciated that when this man gave you his word, he would keep it one way or the other.

She was certain she was falling in love with him. Brenda was right; Cadman Benson was a nice man, and she was glad she had taken Sandy's advice and was getting to know him.

Not that she was looking to put out a line to reel him in, but she was glad he lived next door.

Chapter Fifteen

Three days later, Kasey's parents dropped by her house to visit Dolly. The doorbell rang while they talked and when Kasey opened the door, it was to discover a delivery driver from the local florist holding up a bouquet filled with mingling shades of lavender and white. The arrangement was beautiful, and Kasey's foolish heart hoped they were from Cadman.

Her mother gushed over the beautiful bouquet that included white roses. "Oh my gosh, dear. It is obvious you are on someone's mind. Is there a card?"

Kasey detached the little white envelope held in place by the floral pick, excited to read the message within. However, once her eyes saw the words, she threw the bouquet to the ground and exclaimed, "That son-of-a-bitch!"

Seeing the look of shock on her parent's face, Kasey handed them the card as she said, "They are from Richard."

Her parents read the card, confused. "Well," her mother said, "It was nice of him to let you know he's thinking of you."

Kasey sputtered. "Mother! You know he is a jerk. Why do you think it would be nice of him to send me flowers?"

"I don't know!" Claris exclaimed. She looked down at the beautiful blossoms lying at her daughter's feet and could only think she would gladly take them home with her to enjoy. Not comprehending the gift was a control tactic by Richard.

Before Claris could claim them for herself, her daughter stomped on the petals.

"If I had known they were from him, I would have refused the delivery!"

Her father went to the kitchen and came back with a garbage can to dump what was left of the flowers from the floor. "I wish the man hadn't upset you, Kasey. I guess since you changed your phone number, he found some other way to get to you."

"Perhaps you should call the police?" her mother suggested.

"And tell them what?"

Ed and Claris glanced at each other. Their daughter was right. No crime had been committed.

Bending down, Kasey began tossing the crushed flowers into the trash. She thought the final divorce papers and moving away from California would be the end of Richard controlling her life. Why did the biggest mistake of them all continue to haunt her?

Kasey wished Cadman were home so she could tell him about the unwelcome flowers. While she didn't know how he would handle the situation, she knew his presence alone would make her feel less hopeless.

Once the flowers were in the trash, she tied the bag closed and set it by the back door. The sooner they were out of her house, the better.

"If it happens again," her father said, "maybe you should contact your lawyer and file a harassment suit against him."

Kasey shrugged. "I can ask him, but I doubt there would be adequate grounds to file harassment charges. Richard did not threaten me, and the note only said he was thinking of me."

"Well, I think you should at least contact the lawyer. It never hurts to ask questions."

Half an hour later, Kasey was opening her front door to say goodbye to her parents and promised she would follow through with a call for legal advice.

As she waved her parents off, her eyes drifted to Cadman's house, wishing again that he was home. There was no sign of him or Mutt's return. She closed the door with sadness in her heart.

"Shake it off, Kasey," she told herself, then shook her head. Now she was talking to herself instead of her cat.

She headed into the living room to read for a little while.

The phone rang just as she settled into the recliner.

Staring at the phone, she debated if she wanted to answer it. Even though she had changed her phone number, she wondered if it would be Richard on the line.

With a sigh, she picked up the receiver, ready to slam it back down if she heard her ex's voice on the line.

"Hello?"

"Hey, Sis," Brenda said. "Brett and I are having a picnic in the park this weekend, and we wanted to invite you. We are doing a family thing, you know. Mom and dad are coming, and so are Malcolm and Anita with the kids. Uncle Henry and Aunt Rosa will be in town, so we thought it would be a perfect time to get the family all together. Dad already told me you have the weekend off, so what do you say?"

Kasey thought a family get together might just be the thing to change her mood. She and Brenda might not be close, but they loved each other. Kasey adored her nieces and nephews, so being able to spend time with them was a bonus. There would be a playground nearby for the active kids to wear off their energy. It all sounded like fun. She had not seen her Aunt and Uncle in a very long time.

"Count me in," Kasey said. "What do you want me to bring?"

"Could you bring the paper plates, plastic ware, cups, napkins? You know, any of those things you think we could use. Oh, and bring a dessert? Mom and Anita are bringing hot dishes."

"Sure. I can do that. Just tell me where and what time Saturday and I'll be there."

After Brenda gave her the details, Kasey hung up the phone, found a notepad and pen and began to make a list of the supplies she needed to shop for.

* * *

By the time Friday night arrived, Kasey was exhausted. The moment she arrived home from work, she kicked off her shoes and practically collapsed onto the sofa. For some reason, the store was busier than usual today. Maybe the sale on fertilizer contributed to part of the craziness. People were hell-bent on feeding their lawn nutrients to enhance its growth, but they would bitch when they had to mow the healthy lawn they created.

Dolly came out from one bedroom, advancing with the sway of royalty that only a feline could master. The cat stopped a foot away and stared at her.

Kasey groaned, knowing the big ball of fur expected to be fed.

"You have to wait for a bit. I'm pooped."

The cat's head tilted up in what could only be described as arrogance.

"You won't starve to death, I promise. Besides, I'm sure there is still food in your dish." She could never figure out why cats could not seem to see the food they left in their bowl.

"Meow."

"Meow yourself. If you are in that big of a hurry, you can get it yourself. You know where it is."

Instead of walking away, Dolly jumped into Kasey's lap.

Twenty-eight pounds of fluff kneaded and pawed Kasey's dress until it satisfied the cat enough to lie down.

The knock at Kasey's front door caused her to groan. She was not expecting anyone, and her feet protested at the thought of having to tolerate another moment of torment.

A voice filtered through the open window, followed immediately by a second knock on the door. "Hey Kasey, I know you're home. I can see that Plymouth Roadrunner of yours in the driveway, and your lights are on in the house.

She felt her heart skip a beat when she recognized the voice.

She could not believe the effect of hearing Cadman's baritone had on her.

Her legs seemed to find a life of their own as they immediately sprang to the floor as she quickly stood up. She hesitated for a moment, standing next to the couch as she smoothed her clothing before walking to the front door.

Dolly hissed, showing her displeasure for being rudely launched from the comfort she found in the warm lap. Ignoring Dolly's protest, Kasey opened the door to greet Cadman with a smile. "Hi, neighbor."

Her mouth watered as she looked at him standing in the doorway. He was dressed in a pair of faded blue denim that seemed tailor-made for him. The material gripped around his powerful-looking legs. The black T-shirt he wore stretched over his chest. The logo this time on the front of the shirt read, The F & L Ranch - Get To The Heart of the Badlands Today. There was a silhouette of a horse and rider in the center of the words. The snakeskin cowboy boots covering Cadman's feet were the icing on the cake.

He was sex on legs, and although she was not looking to date anyone, she was not dead. That bulge behind his zipper made her hot.

"Kasey, if you wouldn't mind. I'd appreciate it if you'd look at something else."

Her eyes snapped up to his face as she felt the heat of embarrassment rush to her face. "I, Umm," she nervously bit her lip, "Nice boots," she said, hoping he believed her and had no idea the self-control it took Cadman not to ravish her on the spot.

He could not help his laugh. They both knew she had not been looking at his boots.

"So," he said, at last, trying to ignore the instant lust he felt when she had swung open the door. She was breathtaking beautiful standing in her bare feet, wearing a light golden dress that hung just above her sexy tan knees. Her layered feathered hair framed her long-angular face. The small beauty mark on the side of her mouth turned him on. Although he wanted more than anything to kiss her gorgeous lips, he did not give in to the urge.

His male desires protested at the resolve.

She had been on his mind the whole time he was gone. The moment he returned home, he immediately rushed through a shower and found himself standing on her porch before he realized he had knocked at her door.

He had to say something. The first thing he thought of was, "I just got back, and I was feeling hungry, but I did not want to cook myself anything."

Her eyes narrowed, and she thought to herself… of all the nerve. "You expect me to cook for you?!" She exclaimed indignantly.

His eyes widened. "What? No!" He held up his hands as though he might need to defend himself. "Hell, no! I was going out to grab something to eat but wasn't looking forward to eating by myself so, if you like Chinese, you're welcome to tag along with me."

He told himself that he absolutely was not asking her on a date. This would be two neighbors having a meal together in a public place. It was as simple as that.

"Oh," Kasey was stunned and thrilled at the same time. She was not looking forward to cooking, either. The thought of spending another evening with Cadman Benson appealed to her on so many levels. Even the ones she was not ready to explore.

Suddenly her feet did not hurt so much anymore.

"I'd love to," she said, that wide as Texas smile spreading across her face. "I'll just put on my shoes and grab my purse. I happen to like Chinese food."

A loud and angry meow sounded, and Kasey laughed. "I think I had better feed Dolly first." She turned around and walked to the kitchen. As she did, Cadman could not help eyeing her long slender legs and wondered what they would feel like wrapped around him.

Get those thoughts out of your head, he told himself but could not help the fact his groin was dreaming right along with him.

Chapter Sixteen

Peking Duck, located south of Lincoln Park, was a local favorite for dine-in, takeout, or delivery. The restaurant had a friendly staff that knew how to please.

Choosing the dine-in option, Kasey and Cadman were seated quickly, handed menus, and left alone to make their selections.

Kasey looked over the menu and frowned. “I have no idea what I should order; half the menu is written in Chinese.”

“Would you like suggestions?”

She stared at him. “You read Chinese?”

For a moment, Cadman debated how he wanted to answer that question. “If I wanted to impress you, I’d say yes, ma’am, then make something up. However, the truth is, I’ve been here often enough I practically know what everything is. Do you want beef, lamb, pork, chicken, or duck?”

“I’ve never had duck.”

Cadman shrugged. “It’s actually quite good. A bit richer than chicken. Sweeter and juicier. You’d probably like the chénpí yā lì.”

“Which is?”

“Fried duck tongues with tangerine peel.”

She could not help but smile. She knew he had to be joking.

“Gee. I was hoping to try those at least once in my life.”

Chuckling, aware she was being sarcastic, he flipped the menu over; scanned the selection listed there.

“Maybe I should stick with chicken.”

"If that's what you want, but honestly, the roast duck is mouthwatering."

From over his left shoulder, Cadman heard, "Cadman Benson, is that you?"

Shit, Cadman thought, recognizing the voice. It belonged to one of the local Task Force members. And this guy would not miss the fact he was having dinner with a lady.

Cadman was not one to invite anyone to join him for a meal, especially not a woman. He had no interest in pursuing a long-term relationship and was too occupied with his duties of monitoring for terrorist activity, apprehending criminals, and defusing bombs to even consider dating.

Which was what he'd done in Libya. Found and defused bombs, with the woman sitting across from him staying on his mind the whole time. Fortunately, he had not blown himself up. No matter how often he tried to push her out of his head, she was in his thoughts regardless of his resolve to tell himself she was only a friend.

His heart and body were not thinking of her as a friend, however. His emotions seemed to have a will of their own, and they liked Kasey Davis-Evans more than any woman he had known in the past.

Perhaps the person who had spoken from behind him was not who he thought it was, and the guy's voice only sounded similar. Maybe he could claim she was his sister? Cousin?

He turned his head to see Ian Peterson and his wife Nikki, closing the distance. Sigh. He knew he could not claim Kasey was a relation because Ian knew he did not have a sister.

Damn it.

"Hi, Ian. Nikki," Cadman greeted them.

"My god. I told you, Nikki. It is Cadman. Man, oh, man. Wait until I tell the boys I saw you out with a…."

Nikki poked her husband in the side. “Shut up, Ian.”

“But baby,” Ian said.

Nikki shook her head. “We wanted to say hi.”

Ian was grinning. “Are you going to introduce us to your… date?”

“Shut up, Ian,” Nikki told her husband, again.

“She’s my neighbor,” Cadman said in a tone that suggested Ian listen to his wife.

Ian obviously was not the brightest bulb because he said, “Well, that’s… convenient,” and he grinned.

“Her name is Kasey. We’re going to have a quiet dinner together, as neighbors. And by the way, I’ve heard there is need of a mechanic in Siberia.”

Understanding instantly Cadman would make good on that threat to send him someplace remote, only because the man did not have a sense of humor, Ian looked at his wife and said, “I think they have a table ready for us, baby.”

Nikki shook her head, reached out, and touched Cadman’s shoulder. “It was nice to see you, Cadman. And thank you for…” she trailed off, glanced at Kasey. “Thank you for not needing a mechanic this weekend. We’re having a get-together Saturday with family and friends and spend quality time with our kids.”

It was a subtle way for Nikki to tell Cadman she appreciated the fact he had approved time off for Ian.

All the wives of the team members knew what their husbands really did for a living. The amount of time the families were separated from one another could take their toll.

Cadman understood the need for downtime. It was why he was looking forward to his own vacation in the next week and a half.

With a smile, Cadman told her. "It wasn't a problem. If I need a mechanic, there are others to choose from." He looked at Ian, grinned. "Besides, he's not that good, anyway."

Ian chuckled. "Ouch. Thanks for that, boss."

Nikki bent down and kissed Cadman's cheek. "Thank you again and be sure to stop by." She reached into her purse for a piece of paper and something to write with. Scribbling quickly, she handed Cadman the little note and said, "Here is the where and when. I hope you'll come tomorrow, even for a little while."

Ian said, "And bring your… neighbor."

His wife grabbed his hand, pulled him along with her as they followed the waiter to their table.

Kasey watched the couple move away, then looked at Cadman. "That was a bizarre conversation. He's your mechanic? Is there something wrong with your Firebird?" She frowned. It sounded as though Cadman needed Ian's profession often. Something did not seem right.

Don't go there, Kasey, she told herself. You are not going to start falsely accusing him of something. Although of what she would accuse him of, she was uncertain.

And then she had a thought. Lowering her voice, Kasey asked, "Is Ian Secret Service, too?"

Cadman wanted to lie. Kasey was not a stupid person. But he was not sure how much of the truth he dared share with her.

"No," he said, wanting to give her that much. Ian was a mechanic and worked for a garage in town that believed he was in the National Guard and would give him time off whenever needed.

Kasey stared at him, and he saw a million questions run through her head. "But, it sounds like you need him often to fix your car. If it's giving you that much trouble, perhaps it's time to buy a different vehicle."

"Bite your tongue. I happen to like my Firebird. It's fast and runs like a charm." Christ. Talk about foot in mouth. "After I've had someone fix it, of course." he added and watched as she raised a brow.

Cadman turned his attention back to the menu and waited for her to say something about that slip. But after a moment, when she said nothing, he glanced up; met her eyes.

"There's nothing wrong with your car, is there." She made it a statement.

He sighed. "No." He expected her to say more, but she glanced down at the menu instead.

"It's complicated," he told her.

She met his eyes, gave him a half-smile. "That's for sure. I can't read this damn menu. How about you order for me, and I can blame you if it's gross?"

She surprised him by not interrogating him about Ian. "I would like to tell you, Kasey, but I can't."

"I thought you said you knew what half this stuff on the menu was." She was trying to keep things light. He did not owe her an explanation, and she amazed herself by not assuming he was a criminal. Now that she was beginning to know him, and they had spent time together, she felt he was an honest person. She was also aware she had not been the best judge of Richard's nature. But she no longer wanted to project that mistake onto Cadman.

And she had been around the military for over twenty-five years, so she understood the government's secrets. But she wished with all her heart Cadman would one day trust her enough with what he was keeping classified from her.

The realization hit Cadman like a sudden jolt: he was in serious trouble. He had met no one like her. She had gone from accusing him of all

matter of things to now appearing to trust him. And she was not drilling him as so many women would have.

"Kasey," he began.

"You do not owe me an explanation. However, I want to ask you one question, and I would like an honest answer."

He sat back, braced himself for whatever it was she would say, and wondered if he could truthfully answer the query. "All right."

She pointed to his T-shirt. "You seem to own hundreds of those Medora shirts. They are the only thing I see you in if you aren't heading to work. I want to know what Medora is."

Cadman blinked slowly. Of all the questions Kasey could have asked, he never would have predicted that one. She managed to surprise him. "Are you sure that's your question?" he asked, throwing the opportunity back to her. He wasn't sure why he was giving her a chance to inquire about his job again, but she had handed him a lifeline, and he knew he should take it.

"Absolutely. Perhaps one day, we will have the conversation I'm most curious about, like what Ian really does for you, and why he called you boss. But not today, obviously. So instead, I'm asking; what's the story on those T's of yours?"

He relaxed and knew she was trying to trust him, and that touched him on so many levels.

"Medora," he told her, "Is a small historical town in North Dakota that has been turned into a destination spot for tourists. A friend of mine owns a ranch near there, and he and his wife are always sending me these."

The waiter came, and Cadman ordered the roast duck for them both.

Once the waiter left to put the order into the kitchen, Kasey said, "Well, that's one mystery solved." She grinned. "I'll save the case of

your Firebird needing a mechanic when it runs perfectly fine for another day."

It was an hour later when they had finished the meal and left the restaurant.

As they walked along the sidewalk toward his parked Firebird, Kasey thanked Cadman once more for the meal. The questions she truly wanted to ask still burned in her mind, but she kept them firmly to herself. Instead, they chatted about the possibility of seeing the movie Midway, the film based on the critical World War II turning point in the Pacific, sometime the following week.

During a lap in conversation, as they passed the little shops along the way to the car, and the streetlights came on as the sun began to set, Cadman said, "Thank you."

Kasey glanced at him, wondering if she missed part of the conversation. "Excuse me?"

He stopped walking, turned toward her. "Thanks for tagging along." He shoved his hands into the front of his jeans. "And thanks for not asking any of the thousand questions that are running around in your head about me."

Tilting her head to one side, she told him, "Well, to be honest, it's difficult not to ask what type of work you really do. Of course, I'm curious. But as I said earlier, you'll tell me one day, or you won't. I will not press. It's really not any of my business."

More than anything, he wanted to trust this woman. There was just something about Kasey Evans that reached into his soul. It was an odd sensation. He had never experienced this type of attraction before and was not sure if he liked it.

He would give her part of the truth, at least. "I do work for the President of the United States."

"But not Secret Service," she stated. "And I figure not FBI or CIA because I can't imagine you'd feel you couldn't let people know that."

Shaking his head, and on a laugh, he said, "Aren't you a little Nancy Drew."

She swatted his arm. "I can't help the fact your job has become a mystery to me, and just because I said I wouldn't ask doesn't mean I won't try to figure it out. As long as you're not burying bodies in your backyard, I'll mind my own business."

With tongue in cheek, he teased, "I ran out of sex dolls a long time ago."

They stared at each other, both wanting to laugh, and both wanting something else.

Before they knew it was happening, Cadman reached out, brought his hands up, cupped her face. He searched her eyes, looking for any hint he should back off and not continue with his intent. But she leaned forward, tilted her face up to his, and he followed through with his desire.

He touched his lips to hers and heard what sounded like a car backfiring.

In an instant, he pulled away from her, reached down, and pulled a small revolver from the top of his boot. He had heard that sound more times than he cared to recount. Someone had fired a gun, and if the scream which followed the sound was any sign, the shot had come from the little store just a stone's throw away.

Kasey allowed him to push her back against the building they had stopped in front of. She looked toward the spot where the scream came from at the same time Cadman did. Within seconds, a person in a ski mask rushed out from the little store located there.

The gunman turned back toward the door. With a gun in hand, the person fired back into the building then took off, running up the street away from where Cadman and Kasey stood.

Without a word to Kasey, Cadman took off after the guy.

Heart pounding, Kasey stared after Cadman's retreating back. She feared for his safety but was not stupid enough to follow him. She may not know what Cadman did for a living, but it was apparent he had reacted on instinct when he'd gone after the robber.

Kasey's own nature had her rushing toward the small shop the gunman exited. People were already gathering outside; someone shouted to no one in particular that they called the cops. But Kasey was more concerned about the scream she heard because if someone had been shot, she was going to, if it was not too late, make damn sure the person lived.

"Let me through, I am a nurse," she said as she pushed her way past the crowd. Entering the building, she found a man sprawled on the ground, blood coming from his shoulder and a woman holding him, soothing him and crying at the same time.

Kneeling down, Kasey told the woman, "I am a nurse. Please, let me help."

With tears in her eyes, the woman nodded. "My husband," she choked.

Not waiting for verbal permission, Kasey checked for a pulse; found one. Relieved, she immediately saw the blood seeping through the man's plaid shirt. Without hesitation, she ripped the shirt open at the shoulder so she could get a better idea of what she was dealing with. There could be a life-threatening injury. The subclavian artery, which feeds the main artery of the arm, could have been severed.

If the blood flow Kasey saw was any sign, the bullet had hit the artery. She needed to stop the flow if the man had a chance to live.

"Help me sit him up!" she told the woman, trying to elevate him. Then, using all her strength, as the man's wife acted as a support for the man's back, Kasey placed her palms over the wound and pressed down with as much force as she could to stop the bleeding, or at least, slow it down.

She heard the wail of sirens outside and hoped one of them belonged to an ambulance.

Ten minutes later, Cadman walked back toward the shop with the assailant in tow. He handed the man over to one of the police officers who arrived moments ago. An ambulance was at the curb, and he assumed its crew was inside the store.

Glancing around, he did not see Kasey. However, he spotted Ian and Nikki in a group of people observing the events unfolding. He strolled over to them and asked, "Have you seen Kasey?"

Ian shook his head. "We just got here ourselves. Heard about the commotion and had to see what was happening." He jerked a chin toward the man being shoved into the back of a patrol car. "You just can't get enough of capturing the bad guy, can you? We saw you escorting him, so knew you'd run after him."

Cadman chuckled. "I couldn't let the bastard get away, now, could I?" He glanced around the street once more, looking for any sign of his neighbor, concerned when he could not find her in the crowd. He was about to ask some other bystander, if they might have seen a beautiful blond with a killer smile, when the ambulance crew began coming out from the building with a man on a stretcher.

Looking that way, Cadman spotted Kasey speaking to one of the medical personal. She had a rag in her hand and was using it to wipe away what appeared to be blood from her palms.

Cadman could not prevent the grin that spread across his face. He had rushed after the bad guy, and she had rushed in to help the injured. They made a great team in helping those in need.

He would not dwell on the strange sensation in his heart when he realized he had just thought of the two of them as a pair.

"Boss, I know my wife will tell me to shut up, but I just got to say, that's some woman you got there," Ian said.

Nikki took her husband's hand, shook her head. "Not this time." Then she looked at Cadman; said, "She might be a keeper, Cadman. She complements you nicely."

Cadman would not comment, but what Nikki said stuck with him as he slowly weaved through the crowd toward Kasey.

She saw him. Smiled. When he was close enough, she told him, "I see you got the fucker."

He blinked. The statement had been so unexpected he laughed. "I did. And I see you might have helped save a life."

"I hope so. He'll be heading to emergency surgery, but I think I bought the surgeon's time as I was able to slow the amount of blood coming from his wound." To appease her own anxiety that Cadman had been unharmed, she did a quick top-to-bottom scan of his body. "That had better be his blood I see," she said, giving a nod to the red spot on Cadman's thigh staining his jeans.

Glancing down, Cadman grimaced; was not going to lie. "The bastard got a shot off before I reached him."

Her mouth firmed. "Then I guess we'll be stopping at the hospital before you take me home."

He shook his head. "It's only a graze. Just a nick. Nothing to…,"

The look she gave him reminded him so much of his mother when she was not happy with him, it had him saying, "Fine. If it will make you happy and put your mind at ease, I'll stop by the hospital so they can put a bandage on it and kiss it better."

She swatted his arm. "Good, otherwise if it got infected, I wouldn't feel sorry for you."

Chuckling all the way to his car, Cadman wondered where this woman had been all his life and wished he had not had the thought.

Chapter Seventeen

Their time at the hospital did not take long, and soon they were on their way back to their quiet neighborhood.

When they arrived at Cadman's home, he walked Kasey to her door and waited for her to search her handbag for the key to unlock the door. Once she had the entrance opened, she stepped forward as though to go in, but she stopped and turned.

"Thank you for taking me out to dinner. It was fun. We'll have to do it again sometime."

He smiled, showing that dimple she wanted to touch. "I'm not sure if I can arrange an armed robbery."

She laughed. "Well, I suppose I don't need that part repeated."

They stared at each other, neither of them wanting to end the evening.

"Would you like to…," Kasey began but found her words suddenly cut off when Cadman reached out, pulled her to him, and crushed his lips to hers.

Good god, this man knew how to kiss. All she could do was wrap her arms around his neck and hold on while he seemed hell-bent on devouring her.

Her heart pounded, but she was not afraid. Her every fiber screamed out for his touch, and she returned the kiss with matching heat.

A groan escaped her lips when his mouth moved to her neck. Shivers went up her spine as his beard tickled, and his tongue licked a vein near her ear.

Something was buzzing. An annoying sound that seemed out of place and was definitely a distraction.

"Cadman…," Kasey managed to say, though she was not sure how her mind was functioning. He seemed to have the ability to turn her thoughts to mush, and he had only been kissing her.

"Cadman," she said again.

"Hmm…." He said as his lips moved to the other side of her neck.

Kasey pulled back. "Cadman. Something is buzzing, and it seems to be coming from you."

Cadman pulled away and looked at Kasey, his expression blank as if her meaning was entirely lost on him. His mind was consumed by lust until the sharp buzz at his hip finally yanked his attention, clearing the fog from his thoughts.

"Damn it," he said, grabbing the pager from his belt, read the readout, and cursed again. "Fuck. Not now. I just got back!"

"Would you like to use my phone?" she asked, trying to hide her disappointment. She had been more than willing to finish what he started, but it did not look as though he would make it into her bedroom.

Damn it.

He shook his head. "Sorry. It's a summons, and a phone call won't do." Frickin', frickin' hell!

"All right," she tried not to sound disappointed.

Surprising them both, he leaned down, kissed her again. "I will call you later if I can," he said, then turned away, heading for his Firebird as he reached into the front pocket of his jeans to retrieve his keys.

Kasey waited until Cadman entered his car and drove away before she went inside her own house, closed and locked the door.

"Well, Dolly. I guess we're going to finish reading that book tonight."

Almost to the recliner, her phone rang.

Kasey wondered who would call her at this hour. But then she realized it was probably Brenda calling to make sure Kasey had everything she was supposed to bring tomorrow for the picnic.

Brenda was one of those double checkers who did not trust anyone to do what she had asked, regardless that they had assured her everything was in order.

Kasey answered the phone, and almost threw the receiver across the room when she heard Richard's voice say, "Hello, darling. Did you like the flowers I sent you?"

"For the love of God, Richard, how did you get my number?"

"We have mutual friends, Kasey. It's easy enough to give one of them a call and tell them I lost your phone number. Some of them are willing to help out with supplying me with it."

Now she would have to change her number again and only give it to a trusted few.

"Could you just bother someone else, Richard, and leave me alone?" If he had called just a few moments earlier, when Cadman was here, she would have gladly let her neighbor take the call. Somehow or other, Kasey knew Cadman could probably scare Richard enough to cause him to cease and desist this continued harassment.

"Kasey, come on. I love you. I would like to work things out between us. I understand you feel I wasn't the best husband in the world. That's natural for someone insecure…."

She hung up the phone. She refused to listen to his ridiculous claims.

And damn it, now she would either have to keep her phone off the hook so she would not have to deal with Richard, or she had to answer any calls that came tonight, and hoped it was not Richard on the line.

Well, she was not a coward. And she was not afraid of her ex-husband. She would just hang up if she heard his voice again. Besides, if Cadman

came back home early enough, she was hoping he would call and come over so they could finish what he started on the porch.

Her whole body tingled with the thought, but as the hours passed, it became apparent he was not coming back anytime soon.

* * *

Cadman entered the White House, walked straight to the Oval Office but was told to wait in the hall.

Interesting. Usually, he was given access, no matter who was in the room. But he could be a good soldier and not complain. He sat down in a chair and settled in.

He heard the click-click of high heels coming down the hall. When he glanced up, he cringed when he saw who was in the footwear. He had stayed off her radar for six months, which was a record for him. He usually could not make it past five before she would call him to her office.

She stopped before him and gave him a smile. "Cadman. How lovely to see you. You've been avoiding me."

He stood up. "Doc Hoover, why would you say such a thing? You're one of my favorite people."

On a laugh, she said, "Oh, I know that isn't true. And you never call me by my last name."

What was her last name? he frantically asked himself. She had been the shrink for Task Force Ghost for a little over three years, and he had dubbed her Doc Hoover from day one because he felt all she wanted to do was suck one's brains dry like a vacuum cleaner.

"Rinehart," he told her when the name came to him. "Doctor Rinehart."

He grinned.

Her lips turned upward slightly. "Well, that's progress. When are you going to schedule an appointment to come see me? I sent a note to your secretary to have him arrange a meeting after you were in Libya."

"Hmm. Mark must have forgotten to give it to me."

They both knew Mark was efficient at his job and would not slack on scheduling Cadman's turn with the team's psychiatrist.

"You know I need to check on you to ensure you're up for continued missions."

Cadman gave her a big smile. "I'm great, Hoover."

"No, nightmares? I was told the last mission was touchy."

"I won't lie to you. I'd rather face someone holding a gun to my face than defusing a bomb, but obviously, since I'm standing here, things went well. I don't need to talk about it."

She studied him as though he were a fly under a microscope. "All right. I'll take your word for it, for now. How's your dog?"

Relieved, the woman would not insist she analyze him, he told her, "Mutt's good. He's gotten used to having to go to the Doggie Kennel now and again, but when I come home, he's still willing to be friends."

"Man's best friend," she said and motioned to the chairs outside the door. "I assume the president called you here, and you're waiting to see him."

They both took a seat.

"Correct, you are Doc."

The woman laughed. "Someone told me you acquired a new neighbor recently."

"Yep."

"How is that working out?"

With a laugh, he said, "Better than I expected."

"Good!" she said, with far more enthusiasm than one would expect. "Well, it's always a good thing when one is on friendly terms with the person next door."

The door to the Oval office opened, and an aid stepped out. "The president will see you now, Mr. Benson."

Cadman rose. "Hey, Doc, take care."

"And you more so. And enjoy your vacation that's coming up. It's well deserved."

Chapter Eighteen

Saturday morning arrived with sunshine and the promise of a beautiful cloudless day.

The first thing Kasey did when she woke up that morning was to look outside her bedroom window to see if Cadman's Firebird was in the driveway. He still had not arrived home last night by the time she had gone to bed. Seeing his car sitting in the driveway put her mind at ease.

She was almost tempted to invite him to the family picnic starting at noon today but thought better of it. If she were to show up at a family gathering with him, everyone would assume they were a couple.

Kasey would not expose Cadman to that kind of scrutiny from her parents, and she did not want Brenda to quiz her about their relationship.

She took a quick shower, dressed in jeans and a loose T-shirt for the casual picnic, and then loaded the necessary supplies into her car.

With one last glance toward Cadman's house, Kasey backed her car out of the driveway. She felt a pang of disappointment that she hadn't managed to catch a glimpse of him before she had to leave.

Well, perhaps she would see him later. For now, she put her car in drive and headed toward the assigned park. It would take a good half-hour to get there if the traffic cooperated.

Cadman opened his front door in time to watch the taillights of Kasey's car disappearing from sight.

"Fudge," he said with a sigh. Maybe if he had not overslept, he would have made it to her door before she left.

He had to leave the country tonight and was not sure how long he would be gone. He hoped the op would go well, and he would be back

in time to start his vacation next week Thursday. The 4th of July was a week from tomorrow, and he always took time off for that holiday to meet up with the Fisher's and Lafayette's at the F&L Ranch in North Dakota. It was an annual affair. He had never missed the event since it became a yearly occurrence ten years ago.

Glancing at Mutt, he supposed spending the day with his dog would be good for the canine. The big lug would head to doggy camp tonight because this mission's time frame was unknown.

"Well, come on, Mutt. I'll race you around the block a few of times."

Cadman opened the door wider, and Mutt shot out of the house like a rocket.

"Hey!" Cadman laughed, sprinting after the German Shepherd. "I didn't say you could have a head start!" He gave a shrill whistle, and Mutt stopped on a dime. It was nice to see Mutt's time at the doggy spa was paying off. The boarding house and obedience kennel plus K-9 Training was everything their brochure promised.

Once Cadman caught up to where Mutt stood waiting for him, the two took off at a human pace.

As he ran, Cadman wondered if Kasey had ever been to the Badlands of North Dakota. Though he assumed not since she asked him about the abundance of Medora T-shirts he owned.

It surprised him to note he was considering asking her to go with him. He had never wanted to bring anyone with him for the reunion. Yet he wanted to share that one place in the world he loved more than anywhere on earth. And he had been around the world enough times to have seen some spectacular sights. The only thing he hated about the Fisher's ranch were the horses. He had never been a fan of those four-legged beasts.

He would not get on one this year, he vowed, no matter what.

When Cadman and his dog returned to the house, his eyes immediately fell on the note he had received from Nicki the previous night at the restaurant, lying on the kitchen counter.

“Hey, Mutt,” Cadman said to his dog. “Want to go to the park this afternoon?”

* * *

Kasey sat at the picnic table with the adults while the children dashed around the playground a short distance away.

Everyone enjoyed the lunch of grilled hamburgers, foiled potatoes, salads, and other assorted foods. Now it was time to relax and let everything digest while the adults visited, and the children played.

If one person asked about her failed marriage, Kasey vowed she would leave the table. But fortunately, so far, everyone seemed to have silently agreed her life with Richard was not up for discussion. Everyone talked about everything from Malcolm and Brett’s businesses to their dad’s successful store. Malcolm’s wife, Anita, spoke about their children and the activities they were in. Brenda, of course, had to talk about her children as though they were the smartest, most enlightened kids to ever walked the planet.

Kasey cringed each time Brenda brought up dance class, piano recitals, science fairs, and what have you. It appeared as though Brenda felt the need to compete with everyone.

Kasey scanned the park. The beautiful weather brought out many families today. It appeared as though every picnic table and shelter were full.

Not too far away, a group of men were playing a friendly game of what looked like football.

Tossing a ball around seemed like a better idea than sitting here listening to her sister bragging about her kids. “Excuse me,” Kasey said,

standing up, "I am going to join my nieces and nephews on the play-ground."

She walked off, leaving the adults. Picking up a stray ball along the way toward where children played in a sand pile, she headed for her youngest niece, intending to talk the five-year-old into a game of catch.

"Look out!" someone yelled.

Kasey looked up in time to see the back of a man about to collide with her as he was running backward to catch a football.

There was absolutely no time for her to react.

The man apparently heard the warning from wherever it came from. In a split second, he forgot about the ball he'd been trying to catch, turned, grabbed her by the waist and dragged her with him as he fell to the earth with an oof.

His back hit the ground. She landed on top of him.

Both of them lay there stunned for a split second while others in the park came running to see if the two people were all right.

Kasey braced herself up by placing her palms on the man's chest.

They stared at each other.

"Do you have a receipt for that football?" she asked him.

Cadman roared with laughter.

Kasey's brother reached for his sister. "Are you all right, sis?" Malcolm asked.

With the help of her brother, Kasey moved off Cadman with some grace.

"I'm fine," she said, wiping at her pants to brush away whatever dirt she may have collected in the fall.

Brett Nord reached out a hand toward Cadman to help him up. "Holy, shit, Cadman! That has got to be the most awesome pirouette I've ever

seen!" As he pulled his former football teammate up, he said, "I see you still have the moves you had in high school."

Cadman brushed at his own pants leg as Brett continued to talk. "Lucky for Kasey, I was able to protect her from a bad fall. Honestly, I don't think I could ever repeat that move again if I tried."

Mutt was barking, dancing, and licking Kasey's hand.

"I am all right," she assured Cadman's dog, and wondered why it was she was always talking to animals.

Cadman looked at Kasey. "You're sure you're okay?"

"Positive."

The group of people Cadman was with were talking with Malcolm and Brett, asking them to join their competitive game.

"Come on, Cadman!" one of the guys called to him. "Game on!"

"I'm coming!" Cadman said, then did something he had not planned. He quickly leaned down, gave Kasey a kiss, and said, "I'm glad you're okay. Maybe when this is over and we're back in our little neighborhood, we could talk? I have to leave tonight. I wanted to say goodbye."

Kasey watched him run off toward the group of men and felt her heart tighten. What had he meant by that? Where was he going? He wanted to say goodbye. Was he moving?

God, she wanted to cry.

How had the man wiggled into her heart like this? It was so unexpected, but he had. If not, her heart would not ache like this.

When Richard's mask finally slipped, exposing his narcissism beneath his complimentary facade, Kasey didn't feel heartbroken, she felt betrayed and foolish. The realization that his kindness had been nothing more than an act sparked a furious anger directed at herself for believing his "crap." Without hesitation, she headed straight to her lawyer to file the divorce papers.

But she had not felt heartbroken over saying goodbye to Richard. Relieved, and ready to start a new life, but certainly not distraught over him. Cadman wanting to say goodbye, left her feeling almost devastated.

Swiping the moisture from her eyes, Kasey turned around to go back to the picnic area and came face-to-face with Brenda.

"Oh, my," her sister said, and wiggled her brows. "I knew something was going on between you two! You lucky girl."

"Honestly, Brenda. What is this obsession you have? Cadman and I are friends."

"I saw that kiss, Kasey."

Well, shit and damn.

Kasey raised her chin. "What if there is? Is there a problem with that?"

Brenda shook her head. "No. But I am jealous as hell. When we were in high school, you have no idea how hard I tried to get him into my bed."

Kasey slammed her hands over her ears. "I don't want to hear this."

"Well, if you're worried I had him first, you can put your mind at ease. I never even got a kiss from him."

Thank God, Kasey thought. "Brenda, Brett is your husband. And he treats you well. Obviously, you do not understand how lucky you are to have such a great guy. It would be nice to hear you compliment him for a change."

And Kasey walked away and hoped her sister would show more support for Brett sooner than later.

Chapter Nineteen

Five days passed before Kasey saw Cadman again.

After the picnic ended, they both drove back to their neighborhood, with him following her in his Firebird. He walked her to her door and stood on her porch while he explained he had something to do for the president that would take him overseas, and he was not sure how long he would be gone.

At least she knew he was coming back. That helped ease her mind and calmed her heart.

And he asked her if there would be a way for her to take time off from work for a week starting Friday, which was now two days away. He told her he would be on vacation beginning Thursday, which was tomorrow. And he wanted her to go with him to some annual reunion he never missed and wanted to share with her.

That request sent tingles all the way to her toes. She would never deny how much she wanted to go with him. She even asked her father for the time off, and surprisingly he said yes.

Waiting for Cadman's return was one of the hardest things she had ever endured. To keep her mind occupied, she insisted on working longer hours at the hardware store. It was easier to be at work than at home when she would see his empty house and wonder where he was.

Was he all right? Had he been injured?

Man, oh, man. For a woman who had not been looking for a relationship, she'd fallen in love with a mystery man.

Richard sent her flowers again while Cadman was away. Once again, the note told her he was thinking of her and wished she would reconsider and come back to him.

She promptly threw the bouquet of Peruvian lilies into the trash.

At least he did not have her new phone number.

Kasey couldn't fathom why Richard was continuing his little game, assuming only that it provided him with some kind of perverse pleasure.

She had not lied to Cadman when she told him she was not afraid of Richard. The man had never shown signs of wanting to harm her, nor did he threaten her. He seemed to get his thrills from stalking her.

Perhaps she should call up his other ex-wives and find out if he did the same thing to them.

The following evening, relaxing in her favorite chair and enjoying a good book, she glanced at the calendar and was startled to see the 4th of July was this coming Sunday.

Where in the hell does the time go? She asked herself with a shake of her head. It seemed as though the older she got; time sped up.

When the phone rang, she answered quickly, hoping to hear Cadman's voice.

"Hello, darling. Have you missed me?" Richard asked. "Did you like the flowers?"

"Damn it, Richard! How did you get this number?"

"I've told you, Kasey. I have friends."

Kasey mentally went through the limited list of names she gave the second new number to. She was fairly certain none of them would have given him her number.

How he'd gotten it, she would probably never know.

"Now, admit it," Richard said, "You still love me and want me back."

"Richard, I'll admit I would love for you to leave me alone, and I want you to go to hell."

"Now, Kasey…"

"I'm hanging up and calling the police, Richard. This has gone on long enough."

"You won't do that. Besides, you like it when I call. It gives you happy dreams about me."

"The only dream I have of you is seeing you gone from my life. Move on, Richard. I have."

"You'll never find anyone as good as me, darling. I understand you felt insecure because I'm better than you in the medical field, and because you know I could have any woman I want. But I chose you, Kasey."

Kasey shook her head. Richard's ego was beyond anyone's she had ever known. "Go take a cruise on your yacht and drown, Richard." She slammed the receiver down, picked it back up, and decided to finally take Cadman's advice and call the police.

That got her nowhere, of course. Oh, they were sympathetic, but they could do nothing unless Richard had physically harmed her. Besides, Richard lived in California. It was not their problem.

Well, as she had thought. Calling for help had been useless.

Glancing at the clock, she decided it was time for bed. It was almost eleven.

She walked into the bathroom, brushed her teeth, then climbed into bed.

Turning off the lights, fluffing her pillows, saying goodnight to Dolly, Kasey settled into bed and tried to fall asleep. But with thoughts of Cadman running through her mind, sleep did not come until midnight.

She'd just fallen asleep when the telephone next to her bed rang.

Groggily, she picked up the receiver. She never knew if perhaps an alarm had been triggered at the store, or something happened to one of her parents.

She slammed the receiver down the instant she heard Richard's voice. Pulling the phone off the hook, she tossed it onto the night table and immediately vowed to call her lawyer when the office opened. There had to be a legal solution to stop this harassment, and she would definitely change her phone number, again.

She tried to go back to sleep. Tossed. Turned. Gave up after an hour, got up, and looked out her window.

His black Firebird was in the driveway, and lights were on in his house. She could not prevent her heart from doing a somersault. He was home. Finally. And God damn it, she wanted to run from her house and across her yard to his door. But she would not do it. The man had been gone so long he was probably exhausted.

But she would not have minded if he knocked on her door tonight so she could take a good long look at him and assure herself he was all right. But he probably saw the lights off in her house when he pulled into the driveway and had not wanted to disturb her.

With a sigh, she decided to let him get a good night's sleep before she knocked on his door.

Crawling back into bed, she took the chance Richard had given up and put the receiver back in its cradle.

Five minutes later, the phone rang.

* * *

It felt as though he had been gone an eternity.

Now he was home, and thankful to be there. Grateful, too, that Mutt was excited to see him, rather than tearing him apart when he picked him up from doggie camp before coming home. After five days, the dog probably thought he had no owner.

That would change soon enough. Cadman had thought earlier in the year he should stop going on these ops, and this last venture reminded him of that.

Let the young have the fun of dodging bullets, he thought. It was time to stay in Washington and run the operation from behind his desk. He already let President Ford know he was retiring from the fieldwork.

It was hell to grow old.

Sitting in the recliner in his living room, Cadman scratched behind Mutt's ears and longed for a massage himself. His entire body ached.

"Well, Mutt," he told the dog. "Now that I will be around a lot more, at least you won't have to go off to the boarding house anymore."

Mutt's eyes were closed in doggy bliss as his master's hands continued to stroke that spot behind his right ear with just the right amount of pressure. It caused pleasure all the way to the paws.

Cadman thought about heading to bed but did not seem to have the strength to move out of the chair. He felt as though he was a hundred and two years old, not forty-nine.

As far as Cadman was concerned, there was not a downside to remaining stateside while his team went after the bad guys. He was looking forward to being home most weekends, and off by five Monday through Friday. Unless something needing his attention arose, he would spend more time with Mutt and have a normal life.

Whatever that might be.

The upside to the new arrangement was being able to spend time with Kasey. She was always inside his head.

Somehow Kasey had gotten under his skin without having done anything except be her wonderful self. He had never wanted a woman in his life unless it was for a one-night stand. But Kasey was different, and he knew it. When he arrived home this evening his first instinct had been to rush to her front door, but her lights were off, and he had not wanted to disturb her sleep.

He had not wanted to appear overly eager to see her. But the desire to be near her pulled at him, even at this late hour.

He longed for her the whole time he'd been gone.

He shook his head. Laughed. He could not believe he had fallen in love and with the very one who had made him crazy with her accusations.

Glancing at the clock on the wall, he told himself he needed to drag himself to the bedroom. He would rather fall asleep in bed than in the living room.

It was one o'clock in the morning.

"Come on, Mutt. Let's find our beds."

Not bothering to hide his groan, Cadman stood up, removing his shirt as he headed toward the bedroom.

Pounding on his front door had Mutt barking loud enough to wake the dead if there had been a cemetery nearby.

"Cadman!" The sound of Kasey's muffled voice coming through the door had him forgetting about his aches and pains. He tossed the shirt onto the recliner as he all but ran for the entry.

She looked upset and relieved all at the same time when he opened the door.

He did a quick glance outside, looking for anything lurking in the dark.

Moving aside, he let her in. "What's wrong, Kasey?"

It took her a moment to respond; she seemed mesmerized by the chiseled chest covered with a tattoo of an eagle with its wings spread out. The tips of the wings touched his shoulders. The words, For Freedom, were written in a banner held in the eagle's claws.

She had never suspected he had a tattoo, nor one so vast. It screamed to anyone who would view it, his love for this country.

And yes, the sight made her knees go weak.

"Kasey?" he repeated. "What's wrong?"

She licked her lips. Cadman wished she had not done that. His groin tightened with anticipation as visions of her on her knees, taking him into that enticing mouth filled his head.

"Kasey!" he snapped.

She blinked as though coming out from a daze. For a beat, she could not remember why she was standing in his living room. She had missed him more than she wanted to admit. But seeing him now, bare-chested and all-male, her first thought had been to throw herself into his embrace.

"I know it's late," she said. "And I know it is silly of me to come over here at this hour, but… Richard keeps calling, and although I've taken the phone off the hook several times, the moment I hang it up, it rings."

Cadman's eyes narrowed. "I thought you told your sister you changed your phone number, and that he wasn't bothering you anymore."

"I changed it three times! And he's been sending me flowers these past weeks."

"Christ, Kasey. Why didn't you tell me? I could have taken care of the little shit long before this. At least tell me you've called the police."

"I did. For all the good, it did me. They told me to take the phone off the hook and go to sleep."

Heads would roll, Cadman vowed to himself.

"I just want him to go away and leave me the hell alone."

Cadman turned away and headed into the living room.

"Where are you going?"

"First, I'm going to have your damn ex arrested," he told her.

Her eyes widened. Did this man really have that kind of power?

Cadman picked up the receiver, dialed. As he waited for the call to be answered, he looked over his shoulder at her. “Once he’s brought in, I’ll personally punch him in the face. This will stop, Kasey. Tonight.”

“That would be fantastic,” she eyed his couch. She could really use a good night’s sleep. Did she dare ask?

She licked her lips and said, “Would it be all right if I slept on your couch tonight? I think if I wasn’t alone, I would settle down.”

He stared at her and wondered if she knew that if he said yes, she would not spend the night on his couch, as comfortable as it may be.

Kasey watched Cadman. When he spoke into the phone and said, “Mountain? Viper. I need you to do something for me tonight.” Her eyes grew huge. Had she just stepped into a spy novel?

Glancing back at Kasey, he asked, “Where does the dick live?”

“As far as I know, he still lives at the house we shared in Los Angeles.”

“Address?”

After Kasey told him, Cadman took the phone and delivered a chilling message: "Pick Richard Evans up tonight, or you'll find your face on the other side of your head." His tone was so commanding that Kasey was gripped by an incredible, almost physical urge to fly to California and arrest Richard herself.

After Cadman hung up the phone, he turned to see Kasey staring at him, eyes wide. “My God,” she said, “what is your job?”

He opened his mouth. Closed it, not sure how to answer, but Kasey shook her head. “I said I wouldn’t ask. You do not owe me an explanation.”

Seeing Mutt looking at her, she turned away from Cadman only because looking at him caused an ache that wanted to be soothed.

She wondered if she should mention sleeping on his couch again. Perhaps he would take the hint?

At a loss, she knelt beside Mutt and began stroking his fur, giving her hands something to do when in reality, she wanted to put them on the ink covering Cadman's broad chest.

Cadman watched her as she moved toward the dog. Her knee-length nightgown was lightweight. When she walked past the lamp on the table, her naked body was a shadowed outline beneath the cloth. He could not help that his body responded to the womanly curves. He wanted to touch, but if they were to build any kind of relationship, she would have to accept what he did for America. Half-truths did not feel right where she was concerned, and if he took her to his bed, he needed her to know who he was and what he was capable of.

He wanted more than just a one-night stand with her.

She had to accept what he did for the President of the United States, or she had to go.

Before he realized he was speaking, he heard himself say, "I am the head of a classified organization called Task Force Ghost. Only a handful of officials know we exist."

She turned her eyes toward him and waited for him to say more.

He ran his fingers through his hair. It was difficult to trust, but he wanted, needed, to trust her.

"My team," he continued, "and I breach areas in the world where uprisings are occurring. Sometimes the people behind those rebellions are a threat to the United States. And sometimes, the president cannot wait for permission through proper channels. When that happens, he calls me. My team goes in."

Kasey's eyes moved back to Mutt, and she continued to stroke his fur as she tried to digest what he told her. She had suspected he was something other than Secret Service, but she hadn't imagined something like this.

As the seconds ticked by and she said nothing, he wondered if she had been listening to him. It would be just like her to make him repeat himself. But suddenly she stood and turned toward him. "I guess I can understand why the organization is kept hush, hush. The government does like to keep its secrets. I know that well enough from having been in Nam. But I don't understand why you're looking at me as though I should run out the door and scream into the night because of what you do for a living."

"I kill people, Kasey."

His declaration stunned her. "Excuse me?"

He slowly advanced toward her, surprised she did not back up in an attempt to distance herself from him. Most women would have run by now. But Kasey was not like most women.

"I could glamour it up," he said, stopping when his feet were a half an inch from hers. "I could tell you, it's all in self-defense. After all, the bad guys like to fight back when we're apprehending them." He shrugged. "I bring some people to trial. But sometimes, when everyone knows the person is just plain evil- when that person has burned villages, slaughtered everyone, including children, my team ends them. There is no trial, only an execution."

Their eyes met and she could see him searching for her judgement. However, she couldn't give it to him. Having witnessed the horrors of war, she had come to understand the depths of desperation and cruelty that some would sink to in their pursuit of power. And how many times had she secretly wished those ruthless individuals would perish, not caring about the methods or consequences?

There was wickedness in the world that only someone willing to stand up for the rights of others, in any way possible, could balance.

She could not, would not call him a murderer. He was a hero.

Saying nothing, she reached out her hand; trailed her fingers over the eagle. She felt his chest muscles quiver under her touch. She was being

bold, but she did not care. She had been drawn to him for months. Longed to feel his arms around her. His job be damned. There had been sexual tension between them for weeks, and she had never been shy when desire was on her mind. His eyes followed the movement, watching the path of her fingers. Slowly, his gaze lifted. When his eyes met hers, she saw his had gone hot, and she knew she had the beginnings of a fire on her hands. Her own body trembled, wanting to be consumed.

Never had she been so aware of a man's sexuality. Never had she desired with a need so great she would crumble if he rejected her. She wanted him in ways she had never craved a man before.

Cadman would not insult her by asking if she was sure this was what she wanted. Without a word, he stepped forward, lifted her into his arms, and carried her into his bedroom, kicking the door shut in Mutt's face.

Chapter Twenty

Kasey's arms wrapped around Cadman's neck as he picked her up. Reaching the bedroom and closing the door, he lowered her onto the mattress. Following her down, his lips consumed her mouth as he stretched out on top of her. She nipped his bottom lip, licked it to soothe away the slight discomfort, and smiled when he growled his approval.

Needing to explore, to feel his skin against hers, her hands roamed over the strong muscles in his arms, and the wide expanse of his chiseled chest as she traced his tattoo. Her fingers touched the softness of his beard and wove through his hair, anchoring his mouth more firmly to hers.

When her lips parted, he ravaged her mouth with his tongue, but she matched the onslaught and was satisfied when she heard him groan.

Or had it been her who had made the sound? It did not matter. She did not care.

He whispered her name as though it was an endearment, then nuzzled her neck, his hot breath sending shivers down her spine. He was doing something to a spot just below and behind her right ear, driving her mad, sending heat to her loins. She moaned, arching her body, wanting more.

Cadman's hands were soft caresses as they moved over her nightshirt, finding her breasts. His thumbs moved over the fabric covering her nipples, then replaced one of his thumbs with his mouth, suckling her through the soft cotton as his other thumb and forefinger continued to stroke the other nipple.

"Cadman," she said on a sigh as her hands moved down his back, found the waistband of his jeans.

"Wait," he said, taking her protest into his mouth as one of his hands moved lower, over her flat stomach and the curve of her hip.

When his hand stopped at the bottom of her long shirt, she held her breath, anticipation building as he stroked her thigh with lazy circles. She wanted to beg him to move his hand up and under the hem of her shirt and was bold enough to take her own hand and place it on his, trying to hurry the process as she opened her legs farther.

The smile he gave her belonged to a seducer. Frustratingly slow, his fingers began to climb. The flesh of his fingers moving the material with agonizing speed. Up, stop, stroke. Up, stop, stroke. Almost to where she wanted his fingers to be. Her hips rocked, her loins clenched, wanting, needing, to be filled.

She was going to combust. There was no way she would survive, but when his fingers, at last, reached her core, stroking once, then twice, before he inserted one into her depths, she arched up; cried out on a groan.

"Oh, god," she whispered as she shuddered. She had never had that happen before, but he was not through with his assault. Quickly he moved down her length, and suddenly his mouth replaced his talented fingers. His hands forced her legs apart, spreading her wide as his tongue slowly licked her clit as his beard scraped the skin of her thighs.

She exploded, keening her release as Cadman moved up her body. Unzipping his jeans himself he lowered them and his underwear just enough so that when he grabbed her legs, wrapped them around himself, he drove himself into her like a man possessed. As his hips pistoned, his hands reached around her, his fingers digging into her buttocks as he lifted her higher so she could take him all in.

Together they peaked. Convulsed. Her cries mimicking his as his body collapsed onto her. His hips slowed; rocked, as their labored breathing slowly began coming back to normal. It had felt as though they'd run a marathon.

When he had enough strength to roll off her, he kept his arms around her and molded her against his side. Neither of them could form a

coherent thought, let alone say anything. Maybe in the morning, they would have something to say to each other. But right now, as Kasey curled into him, they give in to the exhaustion of the late hour and the workout they participated in.

Sleep was instant and welcome.

It was a little over five hours later, at six o'clock in the morning, when the telephone next to Cadman's bed rang. He came fully awake, used to receiving calls at any hour of the day and night.

"Yeah?" he said into the receiver, then listened to the news he received. His jaw clutched tightly with his displeasure. Then he barked into the receiver, "Find the son-of-a-bitch. Whatever it takes. Start tracing his credit cards and find his location."

He slammed the receiver down, wiped a hand over his face in frustration and fatigue. He would not deny he wanted to fall back to sleep.

He felt her touch on his arm.

"Do you have to leave?" she asked, those light brown eyes of hers searching his face.

Reaching out, he tucked a stray strand of her hair back behind her ear. "No." He leaned in, captured her lips with his own, and thought maybe he had enough strength for another round of the most amazing sex of his life.

Kasey wrapped her arms around him, liking the fact he would not leave her, and that he seemed ready to repeat last night if what she was feeling pressing against her leg was what she thought it was.

Whining and scratching at the bedroom door had her smiling against his lips. "I believe someone will not wait for us to finish this."

He gently stroked her cheek, ran his fingers through the mass of blond curly hair. "I suppose not. I'll be back in a bit."

Kasey watched him roll off the bed, slip into the jeans he removed completely at some point during their short five-hour rest, and disappear from sight.

She laid back into the soft bed and thought, "Wowzers!" There was no doubt about it. She'd had the best sex of her life last night, and she was greedy enough to hope more was to come.

God, she could get used to waking up next to him every morning, though she was not fool enough to believe Cadman suddenly loved her. In her experience, men did not attach emotions to sex like a woman did. Even Richard, when they were dating, and throughout their marriage, always seemed disconnected after they had sex. He would do the deed, then watch television or leave the house to go have a beer with his buddies, leaving her frustrated and unfulfilled.

For the millionth time, she wondered how she ever thought to marry the narcissistic man.

After last night with Cadman, she now knew what her lady friends meant when they told her sex knocked their socks off.

She was relaxed and sated, yet trembled with anticipation, eager for his return.

But she needed to pee.

Sitting up, she looked around for her nightshirt. She found it lying on the floor across the room, vaguely remembering slipping it off at one point because she had felt as though she were having a hot flash and hoped that did not mean she was pre-menopausal.

She laughed. More likely, her body had been overheated from the bedroom aerobics'.

Climbing out of bed, she slipped the nightshirt over her head. Fleetingly she wondered how she would make it back to her house, short distance it was, with no one in the neighborhood seeing her returning to her home half-naked now that the night was slowly fading to day. She would probably have to ask Cadman to go to her house and gather a few things for her and hoped he would not mind.

Poor Dolly probably thought she would starve to death since Kasey was not there to give her breakfast.

Once she finished in the bathroom, Kasey went back to the bedroom.

Cadman had not returned, and she frowned. It did not take that long to open the door to let a dog out. Perhaps he decided to throw a ball or two for Mutt, and she was not mad about that. Heaven knew the poor dog deserved a lot more attention from its owner than it had gotten since she'd known them.

Maybe she could make Cadman breakfast, and after they ate, they could return to bed.

She almost laughed, knowing she was not a chef by nature, but ever since that first dinner she made for Cadman, she discovered she almost liked to cook.

Perhaps it took the right person to bring out the desire.

Heading toward the kitchen to search through Cadman's cupboards, hoping he had eggs and maybe bacon, she glanced at the unlit fireplace. She saw some framed photos sitting on the mantle and could not resist peeking at them.

As her eyes scanned the dozen or so images, she stilled when she saw an image of Cadman standing with that French actress, Rosalinda Lafayette. The woman's movie producer husband, Charles, and a young boy, she estimated to be about six years old in the photo, were also present. Kasey assumed the boy was the famous couple's son.

It was easy to recognize the couple in the photo with Cadman. One would have to have lived on a deserted island not to recognize them. Kasey herself had seen a few of the actress's films, loving each of them.

Cadman knew them?

Kasey shook her head, finding the whole thing confusing. The photo was likely a fan shot with a celebrity, but that didn't fit Cadman at all. He didn't seem the type to admire someone just because they were famous.

Her eyes moved on to the next photo. There was Cadman again, this time captured playing ball with the young boy in the previous photo. And another with that boy riding on his shoulders.

There were other photos. Some with some children on horses, one with a boy holding a trophy that read First Place. The boy was dressed in some martial arts uniform, and Cadman was by the boy's side, grinning like an idiot and looking as though he were the proudest man in the world. Kasey could not begin to guess who those people were. Brother's? Sisters? Nieces and nephews? What she knew for certain was that Cadman Benson was as mysterious as he was handsome.

* * *

In the backyard, Cadman threw the ball one more time, and Mutt raced after it, brought it back, dropped it at his master's feet, and Cadman tossed it again.

The call this morning was not welcome news. He should have told Kasey right then that his man in California could not locate Richard, but she looked so sexy laying there, looking at him with sleep-laden eyes, his body responded. He wanted to make love to her again.

At least Mutt's interruption gave him the chance to digest the news he received and gave him time to think about the best course of action.

As he tossed the ball for Mutt, and the canine brought it back for him to do it all over again, he wondered how Kasey Evans had suck into his heart. He never intended to fall in love. Never thought he wanted anyone in his life, and yet here he was, smitten. She seemed to be everything he would have ever wanted in a woman had he thought about it.

It felt as though she were his soulmate.

He wondered if it were a twist of fate to have fallen in love with a woman being harassed by a man? Although Cadman could not discern if Richard Evans was an actual threat to Kasey, he would assume her life was in danger until proven otherwise.

There were two women in his life, not related to him, but he loved them like sisters who had been tormented by a man. A man who, to this day, Cadman searched for but could never find. A bigger than life hide and seek game. His best friend's wife, Jacqueline, and Rosalinda Lafayette had endured torment from a maniac; Rosalinda surviving the most heinous attack of them all.

Cadman prayed Kasey's ex was nothing like Pierre Bellefeuille. A true psychopath who enjoyed torture and rape.

The call this morning only brought back the memories of what one man could do to a woman. Although Cadman did not know what Richard Evan's game was, it put Cadman on edge.

Had Richard been in California when he placed those phone calls to Kasey or was the man here in D.C. watching her house?

Mutt brought the ball to him, dropped it at his feet. "Last time," he told the canine and threw the ball across the yard. As the dog ran off, Cadman went back into the house. Kasey had probably fallen asleep, figuring he was not coming back.

He needed to explain to her she might be in danger. Would Richard Evans go beyond constant phone calls and sending flowers? If Kasey kept rejecting Richards's requests to come back to him, would he escalate; become abusive?

Cadman was glad he asked Kasey to request time off to go with him to the annual reunion in North Dakota. His vacation started today. If Kasey had gotten the time off, that was to begin tomorrow. But it needed it to start today. But, no matter what, he would leave today and take her with him. Until he could discern what Richard's game was, he wanted

to take Kasey off Richard's radar, and the best place to hide someone was in the middle of nowhere.

He would call Colten later and let him know he was bringing someone with him to the ranch.

Entering the house, he headed toward the bedroom; found her in the living room looking at the photos he kept on the mantle.

He shoved his hands into the front pockets of his jeans when all he wanted to do was sweep her off her feet, carry her back into the bedroom and remove the nightshirt she wore.

Softly, not wanting to startle her, he said, "I thought you would have gone back to sleep."

Kasey glanced over her shoulder. Smiled. "I thought you would come back and join me."

He moved forward, came up behind her, wrapped his arms around her waist, and pulled her against his chest. "I was going to, but Mutt wanted to play ball."

As she leaned against him, she reached out and picked up the framed photo of the boy with the trophy. "Is this your nephew?"

Looking at the photo, Cadman relived the moment of pride he had felt when the kid won a competition against an appoint six years older than himself. "In a way, yes. He is my best friend's kid, but I'm like an Uncle to the whole tribe. This photo was taken in Seoul, South Korea, in October of nineteen seventy-four. The boy, his name is Hunter, was the youngest competitor. They weren't going to let him participate because the qualifying age is fifteen. But with some negotiation, they allowed him to enter, and he swept the competition."

"No photos of his parents?" Kasey asked, scanning the pictures once more, looking to see who the parents of the prodigy were.

"No. They weren't able to attend," because, he added to himself, Pierre Bellefeuille thinks they are dead, and it would not be safe for them if he found out otherwise.

Colten and Jacqueline rarely traveled outside of North Dakota, and rarer still, outside of the United States. And if they did, it was usually only Jacqueline, disguised by wigs and sunglasses, with Cadman as her escort and Colten stayed behind.

"I take Hunter to his competitions for reasons I cannot go into right now."

"That's sad. That they couldn't be there, I mean." Kasey said, then picked up a framed photo of Cadman and an older woman. Cadman did not have a beard in the picture, and Kasey decided she preferred the beard over the clean-shaven face. He was still handsome without facial hair, but the growth enhanced his appearance.

"Is this your mom?" she asked, pointing to the photo with the older woman. "You look like her."

Resting his chin on the top of her head, he looked at the picture. "Yes. That's my mom."

"She looks so sweet. I think I would like to meet her one day. Did she like the way her living room turned out with the paint I helped you pick out?"

Whoa, whoa, whoa, his mind screamed. He was not at the point in this relationship that he was ready to introduce her to his mother. Everyone knew that if you took a girl home to meet mom, it was one step away from the altar.

Soulmate or not, he was not ready for that.

"Well," Cadman chuckled. "I've meant to tell you I owe you coffee." Unbelievably his mother had absolutely loved the paint and rug, which surprised the hell out of him and his brother.

Kasey smiled up at him. "I had a feeling she would like it. I'm glad you listened to me."

He changed the subject. "I thought you would ask about my knowing Rosalinda and Charles Lafayette, not about my mother's living room."

She shrugged. "It surprised me, and of course. And I'm curious. Are you related to them?"

"Not by blood, but we are close friends. I am also a surrogate uncle to the Lafayette's son, and now their daughter."

"Their son is going to grow up to be a handsome young man. I can see it in him already. A real lady killer he'll be."

She had no idea how her words struck his heart. The boy's biological father was a miserable excuse for a human being and would not hesitate to kill anyone. Although Mason only displayed a kind heart and showed no sign of being capable of horrible crimes, there was always that fear lurking in Cadman's mind, and he prayed to the universe the boy's sweet nature would never turn corrupt.

"I haven't seen their daughter, of course," Kasey continued, unaware of Cadman's turmoil. "But if she looks anything like Rosalinda, she'll grow up to be just as beautiful as her mother."

Kasey turned in his arms. "Would you like some breakfast? I was going to make something for us to eat when I saw the photos and got sidetracked."

Cadman lowered his mouth to hers. Softly at first, but it turned demanding within moments. "Right now, I'm only hungry for you." He picked her up, began carrying her to the bedroom.

Laughing, she put her arms around his neck and told him, "I kind of like this habit of yours."

Chapter Twenty-One

By noon Cadman had gone to Kasey's house, fed her beast of a cat, gathered up some clothes for Kasey, and delivered them to her.

After a shower, and in fresh clothes, Kasey was ready to face the day. "Thanks," she told Cadman as she came into the kitchen where he sat at the table, drinking a cup of coffee and scanning the Thursday paper. "I was worried I would be late for work."

He glanced up from the paper, set the mug of coffee down, and said, "You're not going to work."

She kissed the top of his head. "As much as I would love to spend the whole day with you, I have the evening shift and need to be there by one. Dad gave me the time off I asked for, starting tomorrow, not today."

He shook his head. "I'm telling you; you are not going to work today."

Narrowing her eyes, she told him, "Excuse me? Giving me the best sex of my life does not give you the right to tell me what I can and cannot do. You might be used to commanding others, but I am not one of your… your…," she cycled her hands in the air with frustration as she searched for the word, "Whatever it is you call the people who work for you, but I'm not one of them. You do not have authority over me, and if you think you do, you best get that thought out of your head right now."

He grinned at her. "The best sex of our life?"

"Ugg, of course you would hear that part of what I just said."

"Kasey," he sighed. "Look, you're not going to work, and that's…." He would have said final, but the look she shot him stopped him. Just his luck to have fallen for a woman who would not let a man control her life.

He recalculated and rephrased his speech. “The reason I would appreciate it if you would not go to work today is that I feel you might be in danger.” He could not believe he was softening this into a request. But Kasey was definitely an independent woman, and he had a feeling if he made it a demand, she would do the opposite no matter what he said.

She stared at him briefly before grabbing a mug and pouring her coffee. Taking a sip, she asked, “What, pray tell, is dangerous at the hardware store? Are you a psychic?”

“Now, don’t be sarcastic.”

She raised the mug back up to her lips while she watched him over the rim. “Then, I am going to work.” She set the mug of coffee down and headed for the door.

He made a sound of exasperation. This was not going according to plan. “Wait. Just wait.” He reached out, took her arm to stop her.

She glowered down at his hand, then at his face. “You have two seconds to remove your hand before I kick you in the nuts.”

He raised his hands to his face, fisting them to keep from strangling her. “Kasey, none of my men can locate Richard.”

Her brow arched. “So, he probably is on his yacht.”

“He isn’t there. They checked it out.”

She shrugged. “Well, I certainly do not care where he is at as long as it’s not by a phone and calling me.”

“What does he say when he calls?”

She took a deep breath, let it out. Talking about Richard would give her a headache. “I told you. He wants me to come back to him because I will find no one as good as him.” She shook her head. “Honestly, he is just too full of himself.”

“Does he threaten you?”

Shaking her head, she told him, “No. You have asked me that before.” She took a step to the side in the attempt to go around him to get to the door. “Now you’ll please excuse me, I need to get to work.”

Cadman allowed himself a moment of relief that Richard hadn't directly threatened Kasey. But he knew the harassment could still worsen, and that fear was a vice around his heart. The terrifying, unshaken images of finding Rosalinda after Pierre Bellefeuille kidnapped her instantly flooded his mind.

She almost died.

“Kasey,” he whispered.

Something in his tone had her stopping and looking at him.

“I know your job and helping your dad out are important to you, and under other circumstances, I would never tell you what to do,” his hazel eyes met hers. “But I am asking you to please reconsider and ask your dad to extend your vacation to begin today.”

His soft request caused Kasey’s heart to ache, and she realized then this man feared for her, but could not understand the reason.

“Cadman?”

He ran a hand through his hair, seemed to struggle with an inner demon. “Do you remember, by chance, eleven years ago, Rosalinda Lafayette was kidnapped?”

Not knowing what that had to do with anything, she answered, “Yes. A little. I remember reading the headline, and the one that announced they found her. I think I remember there was something written about her being hospitalized for a time. But the news was vague on any details.”

Cadman began to pace the small kitchen. The details had not been released because they had been too grotesque. And Rosalinda did not need anyone to know what truly had been done to her.

But Cadman knew.

Arms secured to the ceiling, the blood from hundreds of knife inflicted cuts across her body, a broken arm, a swollen face. She had been unrecognizable, and that had not been the only thing she had endured. Her son, though so thoroughly loved by her and Charles and Cadman and countless others, was a daily reminder of what Pierre had done.

Suddenly Cadman stopped his pacing, walked to her, and wrapped her in his arms, wanting to assure himself Kasey had not been the victim and wanting to keep it that way. It was in that moment he realized he would be lost if something happened to her.

How had she come to matter to him so quickly?

He stroked her hair, rested his forehead against hers. "I am going to tell you something, Kasey, and I am trusting you with another secret." He would not tell her about Mason. Only a handful of people knew the truth about him. Until Rosalinda and Charles gave him permission to share the knowledge with Kasey, he would not betray their trust in him.

But he would tell her some details surrounding Rosalinda's abduction and hoped she could understand why he wanted her to stay by his side.

"You are scaring me," Kasey said, trembling.

"I am the one who was the first on scene when Rosalinda was found."

Choosing his words carefully, without revealing all the details, he told her how close Rosalinda had been to death when he found her. When he was through with the tale, he kissed Kasey's lips and used his thumb to wipe away the tears flowing down her cheeks when she understood the pain and suffering the starlet endured.

"I know you do not believe Richard is a danger to you, and maybe he isn't. Maybe he is just a jerk who likes to make stupid phone calls, but

I do not know the man. I do not know if he has any intentions to harm you, but in my line of work, I have to always, always assume the worse." He moved his thumb over her lips, looked into her eyes, and was honest enough to say, "I do not know if I could bear anything happening to you."

Swallowing a lump in her throat, she whispered, "I will let my dad know I cannot come into work today, and that he needs to have someone cover my shift."

Cadman had trusted her with his secrets, and now she would allow him to do what he needed to for his own peace of mind and loved him even more for making her feel cherished.

* * *

After Kasey finished with her call to her dad, Cadman made a call of his own.

He phoned his best friend, Colten Fisher. Surprisingly, the man was in his house at the time and not out working on a broken fence or attending to some other operation of the business he ran.

"Cadman? I'll be damned. This is an unexpected surprise. I hope this doesn't mean you're not coming up for the fourth of July."

"I've never missed one in ten years; I'm not going to start now. I was just wondering if you would have a room available for me tonight. I'm coming up a day early."

There was a pause, then a chuckle. "You miss the horses that much, hmm."

Cadman shuddered. He had never liked horses but damned if he didn't wind up on one every time he visited the ranch. "Not on your life." He glanced up as Kasey came in and walked toward where he sat on the couch. She curled up next to him, and with his free arm, he wrapped it around her. "I'm bringing someone with me."

There was a long pause this time. "Well," Colten said at last, "I'm sure we can find an extra room. My wife will undoubtedly enjoy the company. It will give her someone else to show the twins off too."

With a laugh, Cadman said, "For a man who hadn't wanted more than one child, you sure kept your wife busy having babies."

"Well, I promised her five kids. After Melissa's birth in nineteen seventy, it took some doing, though I was up for the challenge. Of course, Jacqueline had to defy me this time by having twins. I'm now past my quota."

Laughing, Cadman said, "At least Jacqueline can kick you out of her bed now."

"Hey, that was only practice. The real sex will begin soon enough." A pause, then, "The airstrip is completed. You'll no longer have to fly into Dickinson and rent a car to get here."

"I still can't believe you had an airstrip built on your land."

"It was Charles' idea, and he financed it. He was tired of not having easier access when they visit, and it helps keep the prying eyes from any of Rosalinda's fans down. They arrive in private with no fanfare."

About to hang up, Cadman stopped himself then said, "Colt, let your wife know I'd like to be put up in one of the guest cottages this time, instead of the house." He looked at Kasey; smiled. "One with a single bed big enough for two."

"Umm. Well, holy shit! My wife will be over the moon. When's the wedding?"

"Hey now," Cadman laughed, "I said nothing about having a noose around my neck."

Hanging up, Cadman glanced at Kasey again, saw her staring at him.

"A noose?" she asked. "What does that mean?"

He kissed her, not about to tell her Colten was suggesting there was a ball and chain in his future. "He was joking about horses. He runs a horse ranch located south of that town advertised on my t-shirts."

Kasey beamed. "Horses! I love horses!"

Cadman closed his eyes, shook his head. Obviously, it was the bane of his existence to be surrounded by people who liked the smell of horse shit.

"I'll call my emergency dog sitter, get Mutt picked up. Do you want me to make arrangements for your dog too?"

She glared at him. "Dolly is a cat, as you very well know."

"Ha. The size of that thing suggests something different."

She swatted his arm. "I've already made plans. My parents will pick her up tomorrow, but why can't Mutt come with us?"

Hearing his name, Mutt dropped the bone he had been chewing and walked to her, put his head in her lap, and gave her a sad-eyed puppy look that melted her heart.

Kasey cupped the dog's muzzle with her hands, kissed its nose. She looked at Cadman, a plea in her eyes. "You're gone a lot. The poor thing is lonely. Why can't he come with us on this vacation of yours?"

Damned if Mutt's sorrowful eyes did not turn on him. Guilt was a powerful thing. "Fine. Dandy, but he better not get airsick during the flight because you'll be cleaning it up since I'll be flying the plane."

She blinked. "You know how to fly?"

"Yep. And I own a single-engine Cessna. Now let's get over to your place so you can pack a bag."

Kasey's phone was ringing when they entered her house. She picked it up without thought. "Hello?"

"Kasey! Darling. Where have you been? I've been worried sick."

"Damn it, Richard....!"

Cadman grabbed the receiver from her hand, held it up to his mouth and said, "I don't know what your game is, Evans, but I'm strongly suggesting you back off, and stop harassing Kasey."

There was a long silence, then, "Who is this?"

"The person who will break your neck if you don't stop calling Kasey. Go find a hobby and leave your ex-wife alone."

It sounded as though Richard sputtered before he managed to say, "I do not know who you are, but Kasey belongs to me, and you are an idiot if you believe otherwise."

Cadman almost laughed. The man was calling him names? "Kasey does not want you back in her life."

"You must not understand," Richard said, "so I will assume you are slow of mind. She needs me. I'm the best thing to have ever come into her life."

Cadman rolled his eyes, shook his head. "Dick, do you like pain?"

"Excuse me?"

"I ask because, when I find you, I'm going to break every bone in your body."

Done with this conversation, Cadman hung up on the man.

When he turned, it was to find Kasey staring at him. "Was it really necessary to threaten him?"

He blinked. "You're reprimanding me for telling him to back off?"

She threw her hands in the air. Men and their testosterone. "Don't you think that was a bit much? Going all caveman-like that? Seriously, he has only been driving me crazy with phone calls. He has not hurt me or threatened to do so."

Growling low in his throat, Cadman told her, “And you have to understand that if he ever lays a finger on you, there will be hell to pay.”

She saw it in his eyes, his worry, and fear. He only knew one way to keep her safe. Deep down, she did not believe Richard would physically hurt her. But obviously, Cadman did, and she could not blame him for his conviction. He had probably seen more horror in this world than she had, and she saw enough of her own in Korea and Vietnam.

She wrapped her arms around him, pulled his head down for a kiss. “I guess it will take me a while to get used to being with a Neanderthal, but I realize it’s your way, so I’ll try to accept it. Just don’t ever pound your chest and tell me what to do.”

Cadman’s arms encircled her, kissed her back. “I’d never dream of it.”

They chuckled and knew it for the lie it was. But he had already proven he was flexible enough to allow her to be the woman she was.

Chapter Twenty-Two

The couple left Washington D.C. around three in the afternoon. Cadman's single-engine six-passenger Cessna plane had plenty of room for their luggage. They strapped Mutt into the seat directly behind Cadman, so Kasey, in the passenger seat, could keep her eye on him.

Surprisingly, the animal seemed happy as a lark during the four-and-a-half-hour flight to the Fisher Ranch twenty miles south of Medora, North Dakota. The canine would watch the clouds go by for a while, then lay down in the seat as though this was a regular routine.

As they grew closer to their destination and the landscape of the Badlands came into view, Kasey marveled at the beauty of the land. When, only moments earlier, there had been nothing but flat fields of corn and grass below them, abruptly there were sharp walls of rocks and hills and valleys in all shapes and sizes. Colors of light reds and browns, along with purple and gold hues, weaved throughout the disorganized land.

Glancing at Cadman, she asked, "Why are these called the badlands? I see only beauty here."

This area was stunning, he agreed silently. He might not like riding a horse when he visited, but he never tired of the scenery.

Once the plane was on the ground, landing on the newly installed airfield, Cadman taxied the aircraft to an area off the strip to a spot where one or two more small crafts could be strapped down.

He would thank Charles Sunday morning, when the Lafayette's arrived, for this addition to the ranch. This airstrip gave a whole new meaning to the word convenient.

Once the motor was cut, and the blades stopped spinning, Cadman opened the door of the plane. When he glanced up, it was to see three

young people running toward him, followed by a twenty-one-year-old. It was hard to fathom where the years were disappearing to. Clinton, Colten's oldest son, had reached the age of twenty-one only a few months ago; it felt as though the boy should still be only seven, not growing into a man. Following him was the Fisher's oldest girl, Donna, now the tender age of fourteen, along with eleven-year-old Hunter, and six-year-old Melissa.

"Uncle Cadman!" the merry band of troublemakers shouted, waving their arms.

Cadman turned to Kasey, helped her alight from the plane, then turned back to the group just in time to be pounced upon by one and all. They laughed and giggled as Cadman tickled and hugged each one. He loved these kids as though they were his own. His relationship with them more than made up for what his mother thought was a failure on his part to give her grandbabies.

Donna was the first to spot Kasey. "Hi, and wow. Uncle Cadman has never brought a woman here before."

Kasey stood up straight, sort of did a happy wiggle of her shoulders, and could not describe how special that statement made her feel.

Melissa was climbing into the plane. "Uncle Cadman brought a dog!" She squealed her delight.

"Really?" Donna glanced at Cadman, waited for permission before entering the plane to see for herself if what her little sister had said was true.

At Cadman's nod, she bolted into the plane and disappeared from sight.

"Oh, my God!" they all heard Donna exclaim from inside the small craft, "He's adorable!"

Kasey reached out, hooked her arm through Cadman's. With a smile on her lips, she looked up into Cadman's face and chuckled. "I think

Mutt will not know what to do with himself with all the attention I have a feeling he's going to get."

Chuckling, leaving Mutt to the care of the Fisher girls, he opened the cargo hold. Handing the bags to Clinton and Hunter, he took Kasey's hand in his and began walking toward where a car was parked on the other side of the taxiway.

"Well, Hunter," he said to the boy who silently walked beside them, "anything new you want to tell me?"

"Nope."

Typical Hunter. "Your dad says you get to skip three grades this year."

He shrugged. "Schools easy."

Boy, Cadman thought, if that were only true for most people.

"Three grades?" Kasey could not wrap her head around that. Apparently, she must have heard wrong.

"Yes," Cadman told her. "I will tell you about it later."

His attention moved back to Hunter, "Anything else?" he asked him.

"Umm. Nope."

Chuckling, Cadman said, "I understand you recently did a three-mile run in just under seventeen minutes. That is damn good, kid. When I was in the Marines, I did it in eighteen minutes and forty seconds."

"Yeah? Not bad for an old guy."

Cadman laughed.

Kasey marveled at the accomplishment. Three miles in less time than it took her to run a half of one. Was this Superman Jr?

She laughed at her own joke. "Are you training for a marathon?" she asked Hunter.

The eleven-year-old shook his head no.

"Hunter enjoys athletics. Remember that photo you saw at my place this morning? The kid with the trophy? That's him." His chest puffed up with pride as he said, "He's already top ranking in martial arts around the globe."

Without thinking if it were wise, Cadman moved, intending to put the kid in a headlock in a show of manly affection.

In the blink of an eye, Cadman found himself on his back; the air knocked from his lungs.

Kasey gasped. "Cadman!" She didn't know if she should laugh or be concerned. Good lord, that kid was fast, and maybe her earlier thought about the teenager being a young Superman had not been wrong.

Donna and Melissa walked by with Mutt in tow, as though it was not unusual to see Cadman lying on his back on the ground.

As Clinton walked past, he told his younger brother, "Mom's not going to be happy about that."

To his credit, Hunter looked sheepish. He was not looking forward to that conversation with his mother. "Sorry, Uncle Cadman," he said as he offered a hand to help Cadman up.

Thankful that his diaphragm stopped its spasm, and he could pull breath back into his lungs, Cadman told him, "My fault," he took in a couple more deep breaths; his back hurt like a son-of-a-bitch. But he suffered far worst when in the field doing hand-to-hand combat. "I know better." He made his way vertically, brushed his pants off, and, all the while, hoped Hunter would choose a military career. The boy would be a significant asset to Task Force Ghost.

They reached the vehicle with no more mishaps, and, with Clinton at the wheel of the car, they headed toward the Fisher's home less than a quarter mile away.

When the vehicle crested a hill, and the lay of the land was unobstructed, Kasey marveled at the view. Not only because the badlands surrounded the place, but it looked as though there was a small village nestled in the center of the harsh land. Horse stables, a bunkhouse, and barns spread out before them. There was also, what Kasey would learn later, an eating hall, used to feed the ranch help, and any tourist who came for a horseback adventure. There was a small store, next to the eatery, that sold souvenirs and items visitors might want to purchase, or rent, for whatever horseback tour they opted in for. There was an area of about twelve cabins, used by the summer help, or rented to tourists who were looking to stay overnight.

"How big is this spread?" Kasey wondered out loud.

"It's a little over five thousand acres," Cadman answered. "Colten inherited most of the land from his grandfather. A few other acres he purchased over the years as his business grew, and locals wanted to sell."

"Wow," was the only word Kasey could manage to say. But when she saw the main house, the one where the Fisher clan lived, she was dumbstruck. It was a beautiful three-story that looked as though it could be found in the Beverly Hills of California, proudly owned by the rich and famous. Surprisingly, the house blended into the surrounding landscape of the Badlands nicely.

Kasey would have never suspected such a place existed here in this rugged land.

The moment the car came to a halt in the house's driveway, just outside of the four-car garage, the front door of the house was swinging open, and a woman was rushing out.

"Brace yourself, Uncle Cadman," Donna said, "Mom's been dying to meet your fiancée ever since dad told her you have one."

Cadman did not have time to confirm or deny the claim before Jacqueline Fisher was launching herself into his arms. "Cadman!" Good god, she had tears in her eyes, "You have no idea how happy I am for you!"

He managed a glance at Kasey. She was staring at him, and he could only imagine what was going through her mind.

He had not told Colten this was a permanent deal, and it felt as though his best friend were attaching a shackle to his ankle without his consent.

Colten would pay for that, Cadman vowed and wondered where the man was so he could punch him in the nose.

Clearing his throat, trying to dislodge himself from Jacqueline, wanting to explain, yet he did not want to hurt Kasey because damn it, he did love her. But this marriage business was not part of the picture.

Surprisingly, it was Kasey who stepped forward; extended her hand. "Hi, I'm Kasey Evans. Cadman and I…, we're just friends, and I assure you, we are not engaged."

Well damn it, Kasey just saved him from hurting her feelings by setting the record straight, but now he felt jilted. "A little more than friends, Kasey," he said, daring her to deny it.

Her eyes widened as though surprised he would throw the lifeline she offered him back in her face. Fine. She turned to Jacqueline and said, "And lovers. He likes me well enough in bed."

Cadman almost choked.

Jacqueline untangled herself from Cadman, looked him in the eye, and frowned. "Well…, umm…." At a loss, she turned to Kasey. "I'll give you a tour of the house and grounds if you would like."

Looking at her oldest son, Jacqueline told Clinton, "Please take their bags to cabin seven. Unless," she regarded Cadman, "Colten told me you requested one bed for two. Should I arrange separate cabins?"

Why in the hell was he blushing?

"The one cabin will be fine," Kasey said and did not blink an eye.

Clinton came forward and said, "Hunter flipped Uncle Cadman to the ground," as he headed into the house with the luggage.

Jacqueline's eyes narrowed, and she turned them on Hunter.

Hunter's lips thinned. He should have known better than to hope Clinton would keep his mouth shut.

Clinton was always forthcoming with wrongdoings. Not that he meant to be a tattletale. His autistic tendencies caused him to obsess over certain things, and it was just Hunter's luck that one of those obsessions was being an informant.

Damn it.

"Hunter….," Jacqueline's tone warned him he would not like what she said next.

However, Cadman spoke up, saying, "It's not what you're thinking. I was testing his reflexes." He gave Jacqueline an innocent grin. "They are perfect."

Jacqueline glanced between Cadman and Hunter. There was a short pause before she said, "That's good to know. But you'll both be cleaning the main barn tomorrow morning before breakfast."

She would not let them off the hook for that whopper of a lie.

"Mom!" Hunter groaned.

"Jacqueline!" Cadman exclaimed in a, you've-got-to-be-kidding tone.

"Breakfast is at six a.m.," she said for Cadman's benefit. "You'll probably want to head to bed early tonight, so you will be up by four."

Jacqueline turned to Kasey. "I'll give you that tour now while Cadman stands in the driveway with his mouth hanging open."

"You're a vindictive woman, Jacqueline Medora Fisher!" Cadman called after her as she and Kasey disappeared through the door.

From beside him, Hunter mumbled, "No joke."

The tour of the house did not take long, though the stop in the nursery, so Jacqueline could show off her five-month-old twins, delayed the journey. For Jacqueline, it was bittersweet to look at the pair. They

would be the last of her children. She was thirty-seven years old, and although fit, she knew to have any more would be a health risk. Colten had been anxious during this pregnancy more than the others, and each of those caused him stress with fear something might go wrong, and he would lose her.

He had lost his first wife during childbirth.

"This one," she told Kasey, looking down at the crib in front of her, "Is Wyatt, and that is Rebecca."

"They are adorable," Kasey told her, gently touching Rebecca's cheek. Marveling at the texture of the soft baby skin.

"May I ask if you have children?"

With a short laugh, Kasey answered, "I do not mind, and no, I do not have children. I never wanted any. That is not to say I do not like children, I just did not want any of my own. I was too career-minded, I guess, traveling with the Red Cross. It would not have been fair to birth them, then leave them with someone else to raise. I was too selfish to give up my dream of helping those in need." She turned toward Jacqueline. "Does that make me a bad person?"

"Not at all." It sounded like someone else she knew, and she thought of Cadman and hoped the man would not find some excuse to let this woman go. They seemed cut from the same mold, and their personalities complimented each other. Regardless of what Cadman might think, he needed a woman in his life, and this woman would be perfect for him.

But it made her mad that Colten led her to believe there was a permeant relationship in the working between the two of them. He would pay for that later, regardless that she knew Colten well enough to recognize he was attempting some buffoonery at Cadman's expense.

Leaning forward to kiss Wyatt's cheek, Jacqueline told Kasey, "Let's go outside. The evening is beautiful, and the sun will set soon. I also expect my husband to be arriving from the last trail ride of the day at

any moment. I like to sit on the porch and watch the horses from the last guided tour, making their way to the barn."

"I can hardly believe the little town you and your husband have here," Kasey told her as they went down the long staircase that opened into the living room.

With a laugh, Jaqueline said, "It does almost resemble one, doesn't it? When we first married, there was nothing here but dirt and rock, but Colten always wanted to open a business like this, and I loved him enough to want to help make that happen. Besides," she shrugged, "I love horses. I grew up around them when I was a child in France."

"You are French?" That would explain the slight accent Kasey had picked up on, though it was not pronounced.

"Yes. And I believe this land is in my blood. I have an ancestor who lived in the area once, a long time ago. Her husband founded the town north of here and named it after her. That is how Medora, North Dakota, came to be."

"Interesting." Perhaps it was more than that, but Kasey could not think of a better word.

Kasey saw the wall of photos secured in place at the bottom of the grand staircase and moved toward them. "You have a wonderful family." She said while viewing the assortment of pictures. Some of the people in them she could not begin to imagine who they were. But she recognized a younger Jaqueline standing next to a man who Kasey assumed was Colten Fisher hanging in the center of the grouping of family photos.

"Thank you. I sort of like them myself."

Seeing a few photos with Charles and Rosalinda Lafayette in them, Kasey stared. "So, you know the Lafayette's too."

"Rosalinda and I have been best friends since childhood, and we share a common relative."

Jacqueline moved forward, pointed to a black and white photo of a man and woman. The photograph was old, possibly taken in the 1800s somewhere in the badlands. “This is the Marquis de Mores, and his wife, Medora. He is Rosalinda’s 2nd great uncle, and she is my 2nd great aunt. Their grandson, Antoine, is our common relation. He lives in France but has visited the area a few times over the years.”

Kasey shook her head, amazed by the story.

Seeing Cadman enter the room, Jacqueline said, “I’m sure Cadman would be happy to give you a tour of Medora sometime during your stay here.”

He knew a command when he heard it. “Of course,” he said. “That would be so exciting.”

Amused by his sarcasm, Jacqueline laughed.

“I’ve been looking for Colten,” Cadman told her.

“He had to lead the last tour of the day because one of the summer employees felt ill. He wanted to be here to greet you, but business is business.”

“I suppose it is,” Cadman said, moving to stand next to Kasey.

Jacqueline did not miss the way he touched Kasey’s hand; took it into his own.

“Shall we sit on the porch?” she asked and moved that way.

The threesome found chairs, enjoyed watching Donna and Melissa playing with Mutt and the Fisher’s three dogs. Mutt looked as though he were having the time of his life, and Cadman was glad he brought the canine along on this trip.

The sun was lower in the sky now, and it would be another hour before it disappeared entirely beyond the buttes. But before it vanished completely, it would cast a warm glow over the land in subtle shades of red and yellow.

"It is so beautiful," Kasey commented, her voice a whisper as though she feared to speak louder the magical effect would dissolve.

Cadman, sitting next to her on the porch swing, placed his arm around her and pulled her close.

Jacqueline smiled.

The first sounds of hooves hitting the earth, and the excited chatter of the tourists coming back from the two-hour ride into the badlands, were heard long before the group of six came into view.

Kasey watched as the party made their way toward the house. The man in the lead sat the horse under him as though he and the horse were one. As he neared, Kasey could make out his features and acknowledged he was quite handsome. She wondered, too, what had happened to his left eye that caused him to wear a patch over it.

The man called out, "Donny!"

Fourteen-year-old Donna looked up, saw him signal to her, and she headed his way. For one moment, he reined the horse to a stop, said something to the teenager that Kasey could not hear as they were too far away, then he dismounted and handed the reins to the girl.

Donna reached for the saddle horn and vaulted onto the horse, ignoring the stirrups. She then led the group toward the main barn, where she and Fisher employees would help the riders dismount and care for the horses before turning them out for the night.

Obviously, Donna Fisher was a master at horsemanship, though it should not have surprised Kasey. This was, after all, a horse ranch.

Jacqueline stood up, met the man as he reached the top of the porch, and went into his arms, and followed the embrace with a kiss.

Looking up from the kiss, seeing Cadman, the man said, "I see you made it." Untangling from his wife's hug, but keeping his arm draped over her shoulder, he advanced; extended his free hand to Kasey. "I'm Colten Fisher, and I'll assume you're Kasey Evans."

Taking the offered hand for the welcoming greeting, Kasey answered, "You assume correctly. It is nice to meet you."

"If you will excuse me a moment or two, I'll go wash up and change these clothes. As you can see, I have half a pound of dust on me. It's been a long day in the saddle." He kissed Jacqueline once more before entering the house.

Cadman stood, stretched, told the women, "I'll be right back and then, I think I'll be ready to hit the hay seeing how I have a barn to clean out in the morning before the rooster crows."

Kasey watched him retreat into the house, a frown on her face. "Is there a tradition here about hitting hay before going to bed?"

Jacqueline blinked, then burst out laughing. "No, it is an expression that means a person is going to bed. It comes from way back when beds were made from straw and hay. People would hit the mattress to make it more comfortable and to make sure there were no bugs inside."

"Oh! I suppose that makes sense, though I never heard the expression before. My family just said they were going to bed. We weren't cryptic about it."

Chapter Twenty-Three

Cadman followed the path through the house to the mudroom located close to the entrance of the kitchen. It was a place the household occupants used whenever they came in from the trail so they could remove their dirty clothes and indulge in a quick shower if needed. Fresh apparel was kept neatly folded in the small dresser in the room. Each family member had at least one full set of clothing stored in the bureau in the event someone needed to change into clean clothing.

Jacqueline did not tolerate dirt being tracked through the Fisher mansion.

Cadman did not knock on the closed door to the room. He reached for the handle, ecstatic to find it wasn't locked and threw it open with a bang.

Fortunately for him, the person occupying the room was the one he intended to see.

Colten stood in the middle of the room, all but naked except for his underwear. He was about to take a shower before rejoining his wife and guests on the porch.

"What the hell, Cadman," he said startled. "You know if the door is closed the room is…,"

Not breaking stride, Cadman kept advancing. He raised his fist and socked Colten in the jaw. The force of the blow caused his best friend to stumble back a bit, but it had not been strong enough to knock him down.

"What the fuck?!" Colten rubbed his jaw. "What' cha do that for?!"

"That," Cadman gritted, shaking his hand to take away the sting from hitting a jaw that seemed made of marble, "Is for telling everyone Kasey is my fiancée."

A grin formed on Colten's lips, his hand covered his heart, and with the innocence of an angel on his face, he said, "She's not?"

"You know damn well she's not."

"Hmm. Well damn, I must have misunderstood."

"I ought to hit you again. I know well enough you understood me plain as day."

Colten laughed. "I was looking forward to your response when my wife congratulated you but was forced to miss it because one of my guides got sick. Pity. I'm sure the look on your face was comical."

"Damn it, Colten!"

Colten waved a hand, dismissing his friend's tirade. "Don't worry, I'll still have my fun tomorrow. I called Rosalinda as soon as I hung up speaking to you and let her know about your intended. She and Charles are pushing up their arrival time. Instead of coming Sunday morning, they will be here tomorrow afternoon."

"You told Rosalinda I had a girlfriend?!" Cadman exploded. Good Christ Jesus. The starlet, a romantic at heart, would be unmerciful, wanting to know when the wedding was scheduled to take place.

Colten shook his head. "I didn't tell her Kasey was your girlfriend. Geeze, what fun would that be? I told her the same thing I told my wife; that she's your fiancée."

"Fucking A, Colten, this isn't funny."

"From where I'm standing, it is."

"I hate you," Cadman hissed, spun on his heel, and marched away at an angry clip.

Chuckling, knowing that was not true, Colten reached out and shut the mudroom door. He did not mind Cadman's anger. It would be worth it if, in the end, his friend would come to his senses and admit he cared for Kasey Evans, a lot. It had been in Cadman's voice when they had spoken over the phone. The man requested a place for two. That alone was entirely out of character for Cadman. And tonight, when Colten mounted the porch steps and saw the way Cadman was holding Kasey close, it assured him his instincts had not let him down.

It promised to be an entertaining week.

* * *

Cadman strolled outside, reached for Kasey's hand, and told Jacqueline, "We'll call it a night if you do not mind."

Kasey would not mention he had not asked her if she minded, but she was feeling exhausted herself.

With a frown, Jacqueline said, "I thought you'd like to visit with Colten…,"

Cadman's hand still stung. "Nope. I spoke to him a moment ago. We'll see you at breakfast."

"After you…."

"Clean the barn. I know. Christ, if you treated your other guests like this, you would never have grown this ranch into a successful tourist business."

"You are not a guest, you are family, and you know it. So, you know the rules. I appreciate you trying to save Hunter from being reprimanded, but he needs to learn to curve those reflexes. It could have been one of the paying guests who unwittingly found themselves tossed to the ground because of some innocent move that had not meant to harm."

Cadman supposed he could understand why she would be quick to deliver judgment. It did not mean he liked it, but he understood it.

As the couple walked along the lighted path toward the cabin, Jacqueline continued to sit on the porch, waiting for her husband to come out and join her. When he did finally arrive, fifteen minutes after Cadman and Kasey departed, he asked, "Where'd they go?"

"To bed," his wife said. "And you probably should head there yourself since you will be up at four in the morning."

Colten shook his head. "I don't have anything on the schedule that requires me to get up that early."

She looked at him. "Yes, you do. You will be helping Cadman and Hunter clean out the barn before breakfast."

His brow raised. "Firstly, I have no idea what those two did to have drawn the short straw, but I certainly did nothing to deserve that chore. We have our summer employees who rotate that job."

"Did you, or did you not, tell me Cadman had a fiancée?"

He opened his mouth. Closed it. Opened it again and said, "Perhaps I misunderstood him."

Shaking her head, standing up so she could walk to him and wrap her arms around his waist, she told him, "That would be the day you did not understand something your old boss said to you. And I can only imagine you are playing some kind of game that only your twisted humor can understand. However, you lied to me, and I felt like a fool when I congratulated him when he arrived."

Colten grimaced and supposed he should have considered how his wife would react, having not been told the truth.

"It was a small little lie," he began.

"You will either join them cleaning the barn tomorrow morning, or you will sleep somewhere other than our bed tonight."

"Hell," he growled, knowing he had lost that battle.

Kissing him, she said, "I love you, Colten Marshal Fisher."

"I love you too. And I think we should round up the kids and read the next chapter of Knights of the Round Table before we all turn in."

It was a nightly tradition at the Fisher Ranch. The parents would read a chapter from a book to the children, or they would have the children take turns reading a paragraph or two so their reading would be enhanced. It was quality time together, and the kids learned a thing or two, which enforced their education as all of them were homeschooled.

"That is an excellent idea," Jacqueline said, putting her arm around his waist and walked into the house with him.

* * *

In the cabin below the hill, where she and Cadman would spend their nights at the ranch, Kasey sat on the edge of the bed. "Thank you for bringing me here," she told him. "It's beautiful, and the Fishers are truly wonderful people."

Cadman shrugged. "Sometimes they can be a pain in the ass."

Laughing, amused, she stood up, and walked to him. The space was small enough that it only took two steps to close the distance. Without a word, she began unbuttoning his shirt and watched his nostrils flare, and his eyes go hot. "I think," she said, raising her arms and putting them around his neck, "you have to get up in about six hours, and it has already been a long day. You and I need to try out the bed before getting some shuteye. Unless you aren't up for it."

Her right hand slowly slid down his side, found the bulge at the crotch of his jeans. Smiled. "Well, perhaps part of you is willing."

"Witch," he said, just before scooping her up and depositing her on the bed.

Following her down, he began nibbling on her ear before turning his attention to her mouth.

Pleasure shot through her all the way to her toes. God, what this man could do with his mouth and tongue.

She felt his hands trying to pull the tucked in T-shirt she wore out from her jeans and helped him complete the task.

Mission accomplished, he gazed down at her breasts still hidden from view by her bra, and he almost wept to discover the clasp was at the front between her mounds and not at her back.

He moved his mouth down as his fingers worked the clasp, spread the two halves of cloth apart. She had beautiful breasts, and he gave in to the need to suckle.

"Oh god," she breathed, holding his head in place as her legs squeezed together and rocked as the need to be filled by him grew.

He suddenly rolled over, taking her with him, so now he was under her, and she was on top.

Reaching between them, she worked at his jeans, loosening the belt, unzipping the fly.

He lifted his hips as she straddled him and began tugging the offensive denim down, off, and threw the jeans to the floor.

She teased him with her mouth and tongue as she licked her way down his chest toward the underwear that still hid that part of him she craved and was straining against the cotton, begging for release.

There was no hesitation on her part in setting it free.

He hissed when her tongue licked its tip, and he almost jackknifed off the bed.

Knowing he would not last that type of sensation, he reached for the zipper of her own jeans. Then moved her onto her back as he slid them off as quickly as possible, taking her underwear along for the ride.

Both naked now, flesh to flesh, he moved back on top of her; moved his lips back to her ear. God, he loved the taste of her. His fingers traveled down through the curls of her sex, spread the lips to her opening, and felt her readiness on the tips of his fingers.

"Open for me, baby," he told her, and when she brought her legs up to wrap around his waist, he gave one quick thrust and felt as though he had come home. Never in his life had he experienced a joining so beautiful and powerful. But right now, he could not think beyond the sensation.

When it was over, and their bodies liquid and relaxed, they fell asleep and dreamed of the other.

Chapter Twenty-Four

Early in the morning, Cadman reluctantly cleaned out the barn. He was not happy about having to do this tedious chore, but he did feel a small amount of vindication when he learned Jacqueline had given Colten the same punishment. It made him wonder if Colten's presence was due to his wife's anger over his blatant lie, where he falsely claimed that Kasey and Cadman were engaged. Cadman did not ask. He was not in the mood for conversation at this early hour, and it did not appear the others wanted to talk either.

Do the job and get it done seemed to be the motto of the morning.

Breakfast at the Fisher's home was always a flurry of activity. When Cadman entered the house, hating the smell of horseshit more now than ever before, it pleased him to see Kasey had joined the festivities at the breakfast table. When he left her at 4 a.m., she had been snoring, and, oddly enough, he found it adorable.

She sat at the long dining room table with pancakes, bacon, eggs, and summer sausage on her plate.

After washing up, he grabbed his dinnerware, stood in line at the island laden with food. The housekeeper, Sarah Harrison, who had been with the Fishers for almost ten years, ran the proceedings like a well-oiled machine. She had helped to create the efficiency of the mess hall where the hired help ate their own meals.

"Sara, as always, you've outdone yourself. It all looks fantastic," he told her, loading his own plate. Looking around at the offerings he frowned. There seemed to be something missing from the menu. When he did not see what he was looking for, he felt the disappointment all the way to his toes.

"Mr. Benson, you have a scowl on your face," Sara told him. "Is there something wrong with my food?"

His eyes widened. "Never!" he declared.

"Then, what is wrong?"

He felt like a child, but damn it, she always had cheese kuchen for him when he visited. People might consider the dish a German dessert, but to him, it was the perfect added breakfast treat.

With a smile, suspecting what Cadman wanted, the woman turned around, opened a cupboard, withdrew a round dish of the pastry, and handed the whole thing to him. "I hid it just for you; otherwise, there would not have been any left."

Taking the plate, lifting it to his nose to take a deep sniff, he told her, "You know I love you. Seriously, you need to come to Washington and be my housekeeper."

The fifty-year-old woman laughed. "Go sit down next to your lady and eat."

He did, and as he placed the dessert down on the table, he looked at the gathered people eyeing his gift and said, "Mine."

"Uncle Cadman!" Melissa wailed.

Kasey eyed the dish as Cadman eased in next to her, setting his plate of pancakes and eggs down and began eating.

"What is that?" she asked, pointing to the item others at the table were eyeing with envy.

"German cheese kuchen." He began eating the pancakes after lathering them in butter and Maple Syrup.

"Kechen? I have never heard of it."

"It is pronounced ˈkuːxən, or ku-gen; whatever floats your boat." He reached for the dish, cut a small slice, and held it to her mouth. "Try it. I promise you; you'll love it."

Opening her mouth, she took a bite of the offering, closed her eyes, and said, "Mmm. That is so good. May I have another small piece?"

Without hesitation, he cut her another slice.

"That's not fair!" Melissa exclaimed.

Colten walked into the kitchen at that point, and Melissa ran to him. "I want Kuchen too!"

Sara told the master of the house, "I saved it for Cadman. My gift to him."

Cadman shook his head. He would not let the poor girl suffer over a silly desert. Besides, there was plenty enough for him to share. "Fine, you can….,"

Colten held up a hand, cutting him off. "Lissy," his nickname for her, "It was a gift to him. What he does with it is up to him. You know it is not polite to beg.

"But…," the six-year-old began.

"Or to argue. If you want to take that path to punishment, I will oblige you. I won't like it, as I love you to the moon, but I will do it; I promise you that."

Melissa sniffed. She took a longing look toward the pastry and debated if a sore bottom was worth the treat.

Taking a deep breath, hanging her head, she said, "Sorry, Uncle Cadman."

"I love you too, little Missy," Cadman told her and planned to give her a slice of the pie later in the day when her dad was not around. What good was he as an uncle if he could not spoil the kid now and then?

* * *

Later that afternoon, when the sound of a small plane could be heard on the horizon, the Fisher children, while playing a game of cards on the porch, began a wild dance, exclaiming, "They're here! They're here!"

As a unit, the four children raced toward Clinton's car, and Colten and Jacqueline, each holding one of their twins, began walking to Colten's pickup.

Stopping, Jacqueline turned to Cadman, who remained sitting on the porch swing with Kasey. "Were you going to come along to greet the Lafayette's?"

Cadman shook his head. "Na. We'll wait here. Besides, I know you are dying to meet baby Daniela since I could not escort you to France when she was born because you'd just given birth to the twins. You and Rosalinda will be emotional wrecks. Crying, hugging, and cooing over the babies. I'll just stay right here where it's dry, and I have the company of a beautiful woman."

Jacqueline turned away, a smile on her lips. It was the first time Cadman had not been eager to see Rosalinda, and Jacqueline knew right there and then that Cadman had been hooked by another.

As the two vehicles drove off toward the airstrip, Kasey leaned into him, kissed him. "You think I'm beautiful?"

He kissed her jaw, then the side of her mouth. "Definitely." More than that, he was seeing the possibility of having a future with Kasey Evans. It shocked him to admit to himself he would consider such a thing. But being here, with her, without distractions, he wondered what it would be like when they traveled back to Washington and began their daily routine.

"Do the Lafayette's visit here often?"

Cadman pulled back, stared at her. "We have a few moments to ourselves, and you are asking about them?"

Laughing, she told him, "If you keep kissing me like that, we will not be here when everyone comes back."

"Why not?"

The dense man. "Because if I were strong enough, I would be the one picking you up and carrying you to the cabin."

He burst out in laughter.

She swatted his arm. "So, are you going to answer my question?"

He touched her hair, twirled a strand of the blond locks around his finger. Why did it seem as though he always wanted to touch her?

"They come once a year for the fourth of July. Not that it is their country's celebration, but they enjoy the fireworks the Fisher's put on for the tourists. And it is a time that works for their schedules. Usually, Charles clears whatever project he has in the works so his wife can visit here."

"And you escort Jacqueline to France? Colten does not go with her?"

His mood sobered. He had told her about Rosalinda's kidnapping, but he had not told her the Fisher's story.

Because he trusted her, he said, "The man who kidnapped Rosalinda… Is Jacqueline's stepbrother, and he believes Colten and Jacqueline are dead, having been killed by a man he hired to do so. He is the reason Colten only has one eye, and because no one knows where the man is; to keep the Fisher's as safe as possible, Colten and Jacqueline limit their time outside of this state. It is the reason I have always escorted Hunter to every tournament that has taken place in other countries. And why I take Jacqueline to France once a year, but never to Paris. I keep her disguised at all times because it is another layer of protection."

Kasey's heart squeezed at knowing what this family and the Lafayette's had gone through, and she admired Cadman's dedication to them.

"It is the only way Jacqueline she can see her brother and mother," Cadman continued, "Her stepfather passed away five years ago. I arrange the meeting place somewhere in France, and usually not in the same location. The same for when she wants to see Rosalinda. I have to keep this family safe. Pierre would murder them all in a heartbeat if he knew the man he hired to do the job for him had not accomplished the task."

Kasey wondered about his last statement. Perhaps he felt as though the wrongs done to these people somehow were his fault, and he needed to make amends? She was no psychiatrist like her friend Sandy. But she considered the possibility that Cadman's need to protect came out of guilt for something he had had no control over.

Chapter Twenty-Five

Rosalinda Lafayette, clad in a long cotton dress that went to her ankles, and sleeves that stopped at the wrist, alighted from Clinton's vehicle. She handed the bundle she held in her arms to her husband, then all but ran to where Cadman stood with Kasey at his side.

Before Kasey knew what was happening, Rosalinda pulled him into her embrace and kissed him on the lips. "I am mad at you, Cadman."

Untangling himself from the raven-haired, green-eyed goddess, Cadman said, "And it shows. Do you kiss everyone you are mad at?"

"Only you." She smiled up at him. "You did not meet uz with the otherz." Those startling green eyes turned on Kasey, "But now I know why. She is beautiful! Congratulationz."

Cadman had a feeling he knew why she was congratulating him. "Please tell me someone told you the truth; that Kasey and I are not engaged."

Rosalinda's smile turned coy. "I am aware you can zleep with zomeone and not commit to them, Cadman."

Christ, he thought. She would allude to the past they shared before she fell head over heels in love with her husband.

Kasey was looking at him and glancing at Rosalinda. He knew she was no doubt trying to read between the lines.

Cadman cleared his throat. "Rosalinda," he began, though was not sure what he should say.

"We will talk of that later," the starlet told him. Then she reached out, pulled Kasey in for an embrace. "I cannot wait to know you better. You muzt be very zpecial to have captured his attention. Now tell me, how did you two meet?"

Kasey flushed.

"She accused me of shoplifting."

Rosalinda stared for a beat, then laughed. "That iz definitely a story I cannot wait to hear."

When she felt her husband by her side, Rosalinda turned to him and kissed him. Then she introduced Kasey to Charles as she took the baby back from his arms and said, "And thiz iz my beautiful baby, Daniela." She nodded toward the black-haired boy wrestling in the dirt with Hunter. "Our son, Mason."

"I'll have the boys take your luggage to the cottage behind the house," Colten told the Lafayette's as he too came to stand with the others. "I assume, as always, Mason will stay with us in the main house?"

"Hell, yes!" Hunter said, then clamped a hand over his mouth when he realized he said it out loud.

The adults let the slip slide. There was a time for punishment, and a time when a kid had to let loose.

"I would like to accompany a trail ride tomorrow, if possible," Charles told Colten. "I have been looking forward to one since we left France yesterday morning."

"I expected you would," Colten told him. "I put it on the list for first thing in the morning as I know how much you enjoy seeing the sun rising over the buttes."

Kasey spoke up. "Would it be all right if I tagged along? I mean, horses! I love them!"

Cadman looked upwards at the sky and asked, "Why?" as though he were speaking to God.

Laughter by all erupted. Everyone knew Cadman's dislike for horses, though he tolerated them because what else could he do when

surrounded by them, and a group of people who adored the majestic creatures.

"Did you want to tag along?" Colten asked him with a twinkle in his eye and already knowing the answer.

"No. Absolutely not. This is one trip that you will not get me up on one of those four-legged things."

That was firm, and when Saturday morning came, Cadman still stood on his conviction while almost everyone else gathered for a morning ride into the badlands.

As he watched Kasey mounting a horse with Colten's help, he waved the group off and went into the house and straight to Colten's office and made a phone call.

His call was picked up within moments, and he said, "I'm checking in. Have you found Richard Evans yet?"

"I think so. It appears he is in Colorado. I will head there in about an hour. There is a resort in Grand Lake he frequents. Kayaking and yachting are something he loves to do, and Grand Lake is where he likes to go for that. But honestly, sir, from what I can tell, from doing a background check and interviews with people who know him, the guy's a jerk, but he does not appear threatening. No offense, and normally I would not argue with my boss when he gives me an order to arrest someone but, are you sure this guy is dangerous?"

Evans was harassing Kasey. As far as Cadman was concerned, that made him capable of anything. "When you find him, call me." He rattled off the Fisher's phone number.

Cadman hung up the receiver, wiped his hands over his face. Was he overreacting? He was not at all positive he was, but when he closed his eyes, he envisioned Kasey's beautiful face battered and bruised, and his heart squeezed tight. He would keep her safe. He had to.

Rosalinda glided into the room.

Here it comes, Cadman thought. She's going to start grilling me about my relationship with Kasey.

As usual, Rosalinda wore a long dress with long sleeves, and he wondered how she could still look exquisite and not wilted in this heat and humidity. It might only be seven in the morning, but that did not mean the sun had not already begun its torment. The makeup she wore was just enough to cover the scar that ran from the corner of her eye, along her jaw, and stopped at her chin. Unless someone scrutinized her carefully, they could not discern the imperfection. If a person stared, they still would not see the mark because she wore her hair in a side ponytail that helped keep prying eyes off the mark.

She wore long dresses or pants, with long sleeve shirts, to cover the horrific scars on her arms and legs that no amount of makeup could hide.

"Cadman," she began.

"I am not going to talk about Kasey with you."

She blinked. Smiled. "That iz not why I came to find you."

"Oh?" Ha! He did not believe that for a moment. "All right. Did you need something?"

There had been a time a question like that would have provoked her into making sexual innuendos. But from the day she had fallen head-over-heels in love with Charles, her eyes never looked at another man with lust in them. She only desired to be in her husband's arms.

Cadman had been happy for her, finding the true love of her life. Although he had been disappointed too. He'd been half in love with her himself, and until recently, those days of being her on-again, off-again, lover had given him happy dreams over the past years.

Until Kasey came into his life, and now he could not recall the last time he fantasized about the woman standing before him.

They shared a mutual bond that would not be broken. No matter that Rosalinda loved Charles with every fiber of her being, Cadman would

always hold a special place in her heart. She wanted him to find a woman of his own and find the same happiness she had with Charles.

"I would like to go for a walk. Jacqueline ezz busy with work the ranch requires. Sara will watch the babies, and zee children are on the trail ride with the adults. There iz a walking path behind the houze that windz along to the top of a hill, and zee Fisher'z have placed a bench for touristz to zit upon and quietly enjoy zee view."

He understood then. She was asking if he would escort her, and it was not an unreasonable request. It was anyone's guess if a tourist or one of the summer help might recognize her, and although she cherished her fans, she would not risk being alone for fear one of them might mean her harm.

It was a phobia she developed after her kidnapping, and he could not blame her for it.

"Fine," he said, standing up and coming around the desk. "But," he repeated, "I am not going to talk about Kasey."

She linked her arm with his, beamed up at him. "Why would I want to talk about zee other woman?"

"I know you well enough."

Playfully, she punched his arm.

They walked up the path behind the house, passing through patches of buffalo grass and sparse wildflowers, including primrose, prairie rose, and sego lily. Sagebrush struggled against the sunbaked earth. Any grass resilient enough to sprout was kept meticulously short. This wasn't just to make the path easier to walk, but was a crucial precaution against rattlesnakes; the only venomous snakes in the Badlands. Keeping the foliage down reduced the snakes' hiding spots and allowed people to diligently watch for them.

The pair were silent as they walked. Reaching the top of the hill, they stood for a moment, taking in the silence and vastness of the land.

As his eyes scanned the land, he said, "They did a good thing, here." Colten and Jacqueline's dream to develop this area so others could experience the beauty of this rugged land had grown beyond the couple's own expectations.

"Oui. Colten iz very good at running thiz ranch. It iz why Charlez invezted in it yearz ago, but haz nothing to do with operating it. He recognized Colten'z golden touch."

She turned to Cadman. "And you, my dear friend. I am happy you have someone to love."

Oh boy. Here we go, Cadman thought. "Rosalinda," his tone should have told her to drop the subject. He knew well enough she would not stop at the congratulation.

Rosalinda shook her head. "You will not put me off," she told him. "Every day, I have hoped you would find zomeone to call your own. It appearz you have. You should marry her."

He laughed, shook his head. "What makes you think I would want to do that? She's excellent in bed, but I don't need a ring to get her there." He was being flippant, and he knew it. And yet, once the words were out of his mouth, he felt ill for having said them.

For a moment, Rosalinda studied him. She was not at all shocked by his statement. Before she accepted Charles' love, she had been known to sleep with any man she wanted without committing herself to one. Now that she was older, thirty-eight, and with the man of her dreams, she had her regrets. But she also knew Cadman was not the type of man to have a string of women. He was already committed to the woman, regardless of knowing it or not.

"If that iz all she iz to you, why have you brought her here? You do not bring women you are only zleeping with here, to Colten'z home. This place is zpecial to you, and you would only share it with zomeone important to you."

Cadman looked out over the land as his jaw clenched. Damn her for knowing him so well. “It’s not what you think. She has an ex-husband who has been harassing her.”

“He threatenz her?”

Knowing Rosalinda expected him to answer, he told her the truth. “No. He only wants her to know he wants her back and that she will never find anyone better than him.”

A frown creased her forehead. “I do not underztand. If that iz all, he iz doing… ?”

For a long time, Cadman did not answer, but then he whispered, “I could not take the chance he would hurt her.”

She sensed there was something laying under the surface of his emotions she had never noticed before. “Cadman-”

His nostrils flared, “Leave it alone, Rosalinda.” How could he explain the unwarranted fear he had where Kasey was concerned? Nothing pointed to Richard Evans being capable of anything other than being a narcissist who thought too highly of himself. There was no evidence the man would physically harm Kasey. Yet the fear he had of seeing Kasey coming to harm was almost crippling.

He would never forget the day he found Rosalinda on the verge of death, and if that happened to Kasey, he would die inside.

He had not been able to protect Rosalinda, and that fact would haunt him for the rest of his life.

“Help me underztand, Cadman. I have never known you to fear. Iz there more? Zomething you are afraid of?”

Cadman shook his head. She reminded him of Doc Hoover, grilling him. Reaching into his soul so she could dissect his emotions and study them under some microscope later.

"You have told her what you do for your government, haven't you," she stated, touching his arm.

"Yes," he answered, surprised he did not deny it.

"Cadman," Rosalinda whispered, "You already love her. But what is it that haunts you?"

Rosalinda was like a dog with a bone who would not let it go, and he exploded. Spinning on the heel of his boot to face her, he shouted, "I told you! To keep her safe! God damn it, Rosalinda! I could' t keep you safe from Pierre and that will haunt me until the day I die! And I promised you I would find the evil bastard, but it has been eleven years, and I cannot even do that! I do not know if Kasey's ex wants to hurt her physically, and I could not bear it if he harmed her because, yes, damn you, I love her!"

Rosalinda cried out. "Cadman! Have you been blaming yourzelf all theze yearz for what Pierre did to me?"

"I am to blame! I should have been more vigilant that night!"

Tears streamed down her face. She went to him, wrapped her arms around him, rested her forehead on his chest. She could not bear to see him torment himself like this. "No, no!" She reached up, placed her hands on either side of his face, looked him in the eyes. "You are not zuperhuman! You tried to warn Charlez and I not to have our party that night. If anyone ezz to blame, it ezz us. We did not lizten to you, but you found me. You saved my life. Pleaze, Cadman, stop punizhing yourself. You do everything for uz and Colten and Jacqueline. You deserve happinez! We all want that for you. Do not allow Pierre to rob you from the ability to give your heart to zomeone!"

Cadman's arms wrapped around her small, slender form, needing an anchor as he fought his demons.

Rosalinda allowed him the silence of the day and would give him a few moments to compose himself.

She needed the stillness too; her heart broke for him. He had always been so strong she never suspected he would carry guilt over what he had no control over.

Below the hill, she saw a group of riders. She pulled away from Cadman and walked close enough to the edge of the bluff but stopped far enough away from the drop off so she would be in no danger of falling off the side. She put both hands in the air and waved them back and forth, knowing the riders probably would not see her. But it gave Cadman the distance he needed to be alone with his thoughts.

Surprising her, one rider took off their cowboy hat and waved it back at her. Laughing because the sun glinted off the person's bald head, she knew it had been Charles to have seen her.

She felt Cadman come up alongside her. Felt his arm link through hers. "It looks as though they're going to head back soon if I remember that route correctly," Cadman said, his voice sounded like sandpaper from trying to hold back his tears.

Leaning into him she said, "Forgive yourself, Cadman. You are the only one who findz yourself guilty of someone else's crime. We all love you zo very much." She smiled up at him, then kissed his cheek. "And, I hope you know the right route to finding your happinezz with Kazey Evanz."

Chapter Twenty-Six

When Cadman and Rosalinda arrived back at the house after the early morning walk, Kasey pulled him into Colten's study.

With a sensual smile, Cadman told her, "Perhaps we should lock the door?"

"I have something else on my mind," she said, facing him.

Damn it, Cadman thought. "Well, all right. What's up?"

"What's between you and Rosalinda?"

He blinked. "What do you mean? We're friends...."

"With fringe benefits?"

Cadman grinned, rather liking her show of jealousy. "Kasey, Rosalinda is a friend, that's all. She is completely in love with her husband."

Kasey raised a brow. "She sure seems rather familiar with you."

He ran his hands through his hair. "Okay. You want to clear the air? Yes, we were lovers. But it was long before she married Charles. There is nothing between us except a deep-rooted friendship."

She folded her arms over her chest. "Are you lying to me? I'm not used to a woman kissing men who are just friends." Especially when she considered Cadman hers.

"I'll tell her to stop if it will put you at ease." He stepped forward, ran a finger gently down her cheek. "It's just her way." Wrapping her in his arms, he leaned in, nibbled her neck. "Trust me when I tell you I'm not interested in her."

Pulling back, she searched his eyes.

He leaned into her, captured her mouth with his. The kiss was hot, demanding, and caused her head to reel. “You’re the only woman who makes me want to do that,” he told her.

Stepping away from her, he walked to the office door, turned the lock. When he looked over his shoulder at her, Kasey felt her blood heat. There was a promise in his eyes that told her he was about to do more than tell her she was the only one he wanted more than friendship from.

“Did you enjoy that horse ride this morning?” he asked, moving back to her, taking her in his arms. His hands moved under the T-shirt she wore to find her breasts as his tongue licked that sensitive spot behind her ear that drove her mad.

“Y… Yes,” she could not think with his mouth doing those lovely things to her neck.

“I’m about to give that horse competition.”

She moaned.

Cadman scooped Kasey up by the waist and set her gently on the edge of the desk. He immediately reached for the zipper of her jeans, his gaze fixed on hers. "You’re the only one I want, Kasey. No one else compares." He looked deep into her eyes, his voice low and serious. "Do you understand that?"

She bit her bottom lip in a mixture of anticipation and nervousness, as he quickly slipped her shoes off, grateful they weren't complicated cowboy boots. To help him with his purpose, Kasey lifted her hips as he smoothly worked her jeans down her legs.

Cadman let the denim drop to the floor. Meeting her gaze again, he unzipped his fly and moved deliberately between her legs. "You didn’t answer, Kasey," he murmured, his voice husky as he waited for her reply. "Do you understand what I mean?"

“Yes!” she breathed, the single word a gasp of consent. She responded instantly, wrapping her legs tight around his waist in a clear invitation.

"Right answer," he approved, his control finally snapping as he plunged forward to meet the deepest part of her.

They rode the wave of lust in perfect harmony, cresting the peak together in a shared, explosive climax.

Afterward, Cadman held her close for a long moment, as his breathing slowly returned to normal. He kissed her gently, a soft, reverent touch, before looking deeply into her eyes. "Only you, Kasey," he told her, his voice quiet but intense. "Please believe that."

Placing her hands tenderly on his face, she offered him her own reassurance: "I do, Cadman." The powerful word love hovered on her tongue, but fear held it back. She knew how most men reacted to the "L word" and didn't want to pressure him or risk driving him away. Still, the raw intimacy of the moment was enough to finally silence the insecurity that had surfaced yesterday when she witnessed the starlet's familiar greeting. For now, she could finally lay that doubt to rest.

* * *

It was an hour after their encounter in Colten's office when Cadman received the call he had been waiting for from the man he assigned to track down Richard Evans.

"I've got him, sir," his man said during the telephone conversation. "We're in a cabin up in the hills of Colorado. Unless you want me to let him go? He's scared to death, regardless that I promised him I was only detaining him for a little while."

Cadman's smile would have appeared evil to anyone who might have witnessed it. Good. Let the little son-of-a-bitch sweat, he thought to himself. "Tell me the coordinates. I want to meet the man. I have something to say to him in person."

After he had the cabin's location, Cadman strolled out from Colten's study; found Kasey on the couch with Rosalinda and Jacqueline flanking her. Kasey appeared to have a photo album on her lap, paging through it and laughing at something on the page.

The three women looked up when he approached.

Kasey grinned up at him, pointed to the photo album, and told him, "This has got to be the funniest picture I've ever seen."

Curious, he walked around to the back of the couch so he could look over her shoulder to see what she was referring to. He scowled when he saw the photo of himself attached to the page taken at least ten years ago. He was sitting on a horse. The expression the camera captured on his face was one twisted into shock and concern because he thought the horse would buck him off.

Cadman regarded Jacqueline. "You told me you would destroy that photo," he growled.

With a chuckle, Jacqueline said, "It is too priceless."

"So, you lied."

"Well," she faltered.

His smile reminded everyone of the grinch when he thought he found a way to stop Christmas from coming. "Enjoy cleaning the barn tomorrow morning," he told her.

"I..., well...," she stammered, then threw her hands in the air. "For the love of Mike." One of Colten's favorite expressions. But Cadman caught her red-handed, and she knew the rules. She'd been the one to put that one on the list.

Cadman's hand touched Kasey's shoulder. "Could we have a moment?"

"Sure," Kasey said, closed the photo album, stood up, and followed Cadman out to the porch.

He wrapped her in his arms. "I have to make a quick trip to Colorado," he told her. "I'll be back tonight in time to attend the musical with you and everyone else."

Kasey returned the embrace, kissed him, and knew she would miss him even though it would only be a few hours separation. "Dare I ask why you are going there? Or is it all hush-hush stuff?"

"My guy found Dick. I'm going to go have a talk with your ex."

She almost felt sorry for Richard, but she also knew Cadman would not be at ease until he had assured himself her ex-husband was not a threat to her. "All right," she kissed him. "And you better make sure you are here in time for the show. Donna's been looking forward to you seeing her performance in the production with the other trail riders."

"You can be assured I won't miss it. This is her first year participating in the musical with her horse. She would box my ears if I was not here."

He brushed his lips over hers once more before walking toward Colten's truck and using it to drive himself to the airstrip.

Jacqueline and Rosalinda stepped onto the porch just as Cadman drove away.

"Where is Cadman going?" Jacqueline asked.

"He is on his way to confront my ex. Hopefully, the trip will put his mind at ease, and we can go home." Kasey turned. "Please do not misunderstand me. It is beautiful here, but I am eager to go home. My dad could really use my help, and my being gone does not make things easier for him."

"We underztand," Rosalinda told her. "Viziting ezz alwayz nice, but home ezz where zee hart iz."

Jacqueline chuckled, "I am fortunate enough to have friends who come to stay for a little while." She turned toward the doorway. "Shall we play a game of Monopoly to occupy ourselves for a while?"

"That would be fun," Kasey said and followed into the house.

* * *

Someone Like You

Two and a half hours later, Cadman was easing the vehicle he rented at the airport to a stop in front of the cabin where his man was detaining Richard Evans. Stepping out from the car, his boots dislodged pebbles; they crunched beneath his feet as he slammed the car door and walked over them.

He knocked on the door, though he wanted to throw it open and head right for the dick's throat.

Chet Trauger, his team member from California, opened the door.

"Well, you made good time, and I don't mind telling you I'm glad you're here." He motioned Cadman into the cabin; nodded to the center of the room where Cadman could see there was a man bound by ropes and a gag in his mouth.

"I've only had him gagged for the last three hours. He wouldn't shut up," Chet said. "First, he would beg me to let him go, then he would threaten to sue me, then he would cry like a baby. Put that all on continued repeat, and you'll understand why I gagged him."

Cadman shrugged. "I would have just knocked him out."

It was satisfying to watch Richard's eyes go huge with a touch of fear behind them upon hearing that claim. The man began shaking his head and was trying to say something from behind the rag in his mouth.

Cadman walked over, studied the man, and could not see what had drawn a woman like Kasey to him. The blue-eyed blond was not impressive in Cadman's mind.

"Hello, Dick," he said, then pulled a switchblade from the pocket of his jeans. He held it in front of Richard's face, hit the mechanism on the handle that released the blade two inches away from Richard's view.

A wet spot appeared at the crotch of Richard's dress slacks.

Cadman shook his head in disgust but would not stop the torment. He inched the blade forward, placed it under the gag, and cut the cloth in half.

Richard fainted.

"Well, fuck," Cadman said. "Now, I have to wait for the little prick to come to before I can have my chit-chat with him." He looked at Chet. "Could you bring a container of cold water and throw it on the guy? I've got an appointment I do not want to be late for."

Chet hurriedly brought a bucket of water, threw it into Richard's face.

The man came awake coughing and sputtering.

"Welcome back, twinkle toes," Cadman told Richard.

"Who are you?! What do you want! If it is money you are after, I can get that for you. I have tons of money. Just let me go! I have not done anything wrong!"

Cadman eased out a nearby chair, pulled it in front of Richard, straddled it. "Well, Dick, my name is Cadman Benson. I spoke to you on the phone a few days ago. It was on the last day you called Kasey. She has asked you to stop harassing her. Now I am telling you, you will never contact her, in any way, again, or I will be doing more than just sit here having a conversation with you." He leaned forward. "And trust me, you do not want that to happen."

"But…," Richard's voice quivered, "But…. I want Kasey back…."

"She's mine now," Cadman said. "And the fact is, we will be getting married." Well, he had not asked her yet, but that was a detail that did not need to be brought up. "Do I make myself clear? I protect those I love, by any means possible."

"I'll sue…." But the threat had no backbone behind it.

Cadman shrugged. "You are welcome to try." He looked at Chet. "Have either of us been to Colorado recently?"

Chet shook his head. "I do not believe so, sir. I have been on the beach in Miami, Florida, this whole week, and I have lots of witnesses to place me there."

Cadman put his hand on his heart, grinned. "That is such a coincidence because I'm there too!"

Turning his attention back to Richard, Cadman asked him, "Have I made myself clear, Dick? If I so much as discover you contact Kasey ever again, or come within a hundred miles of her, there is no place on earth you can go that I won't find you."

Richard's eyes bulged, but he nodded his head. "I swear! You can have her!" He laughed nervously. "It was just a game. No harm. I only wanted her back because she dumped me. Can you believe that? I am a prize catch, and she insulted me by getting that divorce three months after I got her. I usually get the divorce first once I grow bored."

Cadman's eyes narrowed. "How many times have you been married?"

The smile Richard gave him was sly. "I've collected seven wives so far." He said it with pride, as though his only goal in life was to love them and leave them.

Cadman wanted to punch the man in the face. "I suggest that ends now, you little prick. I will be keeping tabs on you, you dick. Any more marriages and you might as well plan your own funeral."

"But…," Richard sputtered, "You cannot…."

Cadman bent down, grabbed the lapels of Richard's shirt, and pulled him toward him until they were nose to nose and eye to eye. "If you wish to test that theory, I would be more than happy to oblige you."

Richard's heart drummed, and he had the uncanny feeling he had just looked into the eyes of death.

"Okay," Richard said, and it sounded like a little mouse squeak.

Satisfied, Cadman turned to Chet. "You can take him back to wherever you took him from. I'm through here."

Chapter Twenty-Seven

At the newly remodeled amphitheater in Medora, Kasey sat between the Fisher's and Lafayette's on the hard bleachers. All the family members, except for the twins and baby Daniela, who were with Sarah back at the F&L Ranch, were in attendance for tonight's performance of Donna's debut in the show. Tonight, it would be the teenager's turn to race across the outdoor stage on her horse, carrying the American flag. Later, Kasey was told, the girl would be spotlighted in the buttes when it came time in the show to honor the cowboys from days gone by.

The Burning Hills Singers, the name of the musical act, performed several numbers against the scenic background, with a featured comedy attraction showcased in between the singing routine.

Donna's part would be half-way through the second act, and Kasey was growing concerned that Cadman would miss the teenager's entrance.

Applauding the end of the dog act, which also signaled intermission, Kasey stood and stretched as many spectators did the same. Some attendees moved into the isles to make their way to the concessions. Others began forming lines to the restrooms on the upper levels of the theater.

The Fisher children, along with Mason, were given permission to purchase some popcorn and soda to snack on during the second half of the show, and they raced off to find the shortest line.

Kasey scanned the crowd, hoping to see Cadman in the mob.

"He'll be here," Colten said. "He would not miss Donny's ride. She'd never let him hear the end of it if he did."

"I hope so. Be here in time, I mean," Kasey said.

Jacqueline handed Kasey a lap blanket and told her, "The sun will go down soon, and you will need this to help keep you warm."

Kasey took the blanket, sat back down, and watched the activity on stage as people slid a few of the movable buildings into different spots as they prepared for the second half of the show.

A bag of popcorn appeared in front of her face.

"I know you like lots of butter, so I asked for an extra amount."

Her heart somersaulted upon hearing his voice. Looking up at Cadman, she smiled, reached for the bag, and took his hand. She pulled him down to the seat next to hers and greeted him with a kiss full of heat.

He returned the kiss, then said, "I think I like the way you have of making me feel as though I was missed."

She snuggled into him, resting her head on his shoulder. "I was beginning to think you would not make it back on time."

"I promised I would."

"And you saw Richard?"

Cadman chuckled. "Yep. I don't know what you saw in the dick, but he won't be bothering you anymore."

The outdoor lighting was being dimmed, signaling intermission was ending, and the second half of the show was about to begin.

"I will not ask how you convinced him to stop calling me, but I am grateful for your help." She spread out the blanket over them as the sky darkened, and lengthening shadows crept over the land.

When most of the spectators had returned to their seats, Cadman and Kasey held hands and watched the show begin.

Donna's ride across the stage was a superb display of horsemanship. Starting on one end of the stage, the horse reared, pawed the air with its hoofs as Donna waved the American flag. Then in a quick move, the

horse landed on all fours and took off across the stage with Donna riding low and kicking her heels into the horse's flanks.

Colten whooped. "That's my girl!" as the crowd clapped, and those around Colten chuckled at a father's enthusiasm.

Later, when the production ended, those in attendance made the trek up the steep embankment leading to the parking area consisting of nothing more than an empty field and prairie grass.

Cadman took Kasey's hand in his as they strolled along toward the hundreds of vehicles waiting for their drivers. He told her, "If you would rather ride back to the ranch with the group you came with, just let me know. But since I'm driving Colten's pickup, and those twenty miles back to his place could get lonely, I would rather you keep me company."

She put her arm around his waist, walked with him hip to hip. "I think I will stay with you."

"Good," he said as they reached the Chevrolet Silverado. He unlocked and opened the passenger door for her, helped her into the vehicle, then walked around to the driver's side.

Once they made their way down the winding road with bumper-to-bumper vehicles, they crossed the railroad tracks, and Cadman made a turn toward the small town of Medora. Instead of driving past the little village, he turned left and drove through the entrance of the Theodore Roosevelt National Memorial Park.

Kasey watched the scenery pass by for a little while before she said, "I realize I have not been here long enough to know the exact route to the F&L, but I am fairly certain it is located in the opposite direction from the way we are going."

Slowing the vehicle for a sharp curve in the road, Cadman told her, "I wanted to show you something before we head back to the ranch."

Less than ten minutes later, he eased the truck off the road and onto a small cutout that had a signpost that read scenic view. Turning off the engine and headlights, Cadman motioned to the area that could be seen through the windshield.

Below them, the last rays of the sun burst across the land; its glow-giving the hills the illusion of fire as the colors of orange, yellow, and red flickered across their faces.

Kasey was at a loss for words. Nature's natural splendor took her breath away.

"I never grow tired of seeing that," Cadman said, breaking the silence when the sun completely set, and only darkness surrounded them. "You will never see a sunset like that in D.C." He turned toward her, flipped on the overhead light in the truck's cab so he could see her face.

"You were right about Dick," he continued. "He's a complete ass, but at least now I know he would not physically hurt you and thank you for allowing me to put that aside."

She reached up, cupped his cheek with her palm. "I knew you needed to confirm he is not anything more than a narcissist who could not process my rejection of him."

He placed his hand on hers. "I also know you want to get back to D.C. to help your dad out, but if you could stay here with me for a few more days, until the Lafayette's leave, I would appreciate it. It's a tradition of mine to spend the week of the fourth of July here, with my extended family. I am also hoping you would make them your family too."

Kasey searched his eyes, not sure what his statement meant.

"Your friends are wonderful," she told him, easing back a bit, and placed her hands into her lap. "They have welcomed me as though I am already a part of their circle. And I believe they have all wormed their way into my heart already. Tomorrow morning, I will call my parents and see if they can manage a few more days without me. If they are

doing all right, and there are no problems at the store, I would be happy to stay here with you for a little while longer."

He leaned forward, reached a hand around her to bring her to him for a kiss before sitting back and letting a chuckle escape from his lips.

"My mother," he said, "Is never going to believe I'm getting married." Hell, he did not believe it himself.

Kasey stared at him. Had there been a proposal somewhere in this conversation? She may very well be an independent woman and was not the man seeking type, but that did not mean she was not a romantic at heart. She would have liked a little more flair if he were talking about marrying her.

Not able to resist, she said, "Oh yeah? Who is the lucky girl?"

His head turned toward her, a frown on his brow and confusion written over his face. "What do you mean, who is the lucky girl?"

"You said you were getting married. I asked you who the girl was." She kept her face a somber mask regardless of the fact she found his facial expression hilarious.

He stammered. "I was talking about you!" he exploded in disbelief.

She shook her head, held out her left hand, and examined the fingers. "Well, if that's true, I do not see the evidence of your intent, and you certainly have not asked me if I will have you for a husband."

He opened his mouth. Closed it. Opened it again. "I asked!"

"No, you did not."

"For the love of...," he turned the overhead light off, and the truck's engine and headlights on. He backed out of the scenic view cutout without bothering to look to see if there was another car coming.

As he slammed the gearshift into drive, he said, "I cannot believe you did not understand what I was talking about when I asked if you could make my extended family yours too."

She folded her arms across her chest. “Perhaps if you would have had a ring to offer, it might have clarified things better.”

Silence stretched between them. His jaw clenched. Females. No wonder he never wanted one to stay in his life very long.

It was not until he turned the truck onto the road that would set them on the path to the F&L Ranch that he managed to find his voice again.

“What was I supposed to do? Bring you flowers and sing you a song?”

“Do you sing?” she asked, enjoying his annoyance. Who would have thought it would be this much fun to tease him?

“No. Unless you want the coyotes to howl, I’m not going to prove my point.”

“I’ll take your word for it.” It was hard not to laugh.

“I suppose Dick’s proposal was as amazing as fuck.”

She had to turn her head away from him, toward the window, and place her knuckles against her mouth to prevent her laughter.

“Well, actually….,”

“I don’t want to hear about it.”

She shrugged. “Okay.”

He looked at her from the corner of his eye. “I suppose you want some stupid white knight on a steed.”

“I told you, a ring would have been nice. I take a size seven if that helps.”

He did not say a word for the next eighteen miles, and when he drove through the main entrance of the ranch, he eased to a stop in front of the cabin they shared and told her, “Have a good night. I will see you sometime tomorrow.”

Perhaps she had taken this a little too far. “Cadman-”

He leaned past her and opened her door.

Seriously? He was that mad about his lack of a proposal? Didn't she have the right to want a little romance?

She slid out of the pickup. To clarify, she said, "You're not coming in?"

"Close the door, Kasey."

Chapter Twenty-Eight

When noon of the next day arrived and Cadman still hadn't returned, Kasey was torn between being furious with him and gravely concerned that something had happened. She couldn't believe he had become so upset over her teasing him about his less-than-romantic proposal. If he had only stayed last night instead of driving off in a huff, she had been prepared to tell him yes, she would marry him; right after she seduced him into making love to her.

But he had not given her the chance, the silly man, and now he was missing. She was not sure if she wanted to ask someone to go look for him or wait. Perhaps he would return by that evening?

No one seemed concerned that he was not at the ranch, so she tried to follow their lead and not worry over Cadman's absence.

She used the Fisher's phone to check in with her parents. Thankfully, everything seemed to be running smoothly at the hardware store. Although they would be grateful for her return, they assured her she could continue to enjoy her vacation for a little while longer. As for her cat, she was told Dolly was adjusting to her new surroundings, which was a load off Kasey's mind, too.

Despite enjoying the peace and beauty of the Badlands, Kasey longed for her normal routine back home. While her daily work involved minor hassles, like absent employees or customers expecting things for free, she kept these issues in perspective, recalling her time saving lives in Vietnam. In contrast to that past, she now found genuine enjoyment in learning about the various pesticides and plant foods that aided her customers' gardens.

Soon after she talked to her parents, Jacqueline and Rosalinda approached her and said they wanted to take her into the town of Medora and show her the sights. Kasey suspected the two women were

attempting to keep her from dwelling on Cadman's absence, though she was not opposed to spending a few hours away from the ranch.

When Kasey described Cadman's proposal over breakfast, Rosalinda and Jacqueline were appalled by his complete lack of romance. They agreed that Cadman urgently needed to learn how to woo a woman to keep Kasey interested, though they worried his many years as a bachelor had made him incapable of learning the art.

Determined to protect Kasey and Cadman's future, Rosalinda and Jacqueline made a pact: they would force the necessary knowledge onto the man. They felt they had waited an eternity for Cadman to find someone like Kasey, and they absolutely refused to watch his romance incompetence drive her away.

The women departed the ranch around one in the afternoon, with Jacqueline driving the family Buick station wagon. Upon reaching Medora, the first stop was to the home Rosalinda's 2nd great uncle had built in Medora in 1883 for his family to use as a hunting lodge and summer home during their time here in the badlands. It intrigued Kasey that the home had stood on the same piece of land for ninety-three years and was still in very good condition, though the 26-room, two-story building had been restored from 1937 to 1941 by the Civilian Conservation Corps after the building and grounds were donated to the State on the condition it be maintained as a museum by the couple's oldest son in 1936.

Kasey enjoyed touring the house, fascinated by many of the original furnishings and personal effects of the de Mores family presented for visitors to view and imagine the life that was lived here during the early beginnings of this area.

From the house, the threesome drove into the town; walked the streets that had a few boarded sidewalks to give the town the feel of the olden days, but Kasey could see that slowly cemented walkways were replacing the planks of wood.

They browsed the shop in the Joe Ferris Store. It was there Kasey learned Theodore Roosevelt once lived in this area, before he became the President of the United States, and this building had belonged to the man who guided Roosevelt in 1883 on a buffalo hunt. The men remained good friends for the rest of their lives.

By five o'clock in the afternoon, the women called it a day and headed back to the ranch.

* * *

Cadman stood in the corral with Colten, eyeing the horse his friend was holding; waiting for him to mount up.

"I don't like this one," Cadman said. "He is looking at me as though he cannot wait to buck me off."

Colten shook his head, laughed. "He is a she, and she is not thinking any such thing. She is as gentle as a lamb."

"Sure, she is."

"Have I ever put you on a spirited horse?" Colten sounded insulted Cadman would suggest such a thing.

"No, but that does not mean one of them won't act up. What if something spooks her?"

"For the love of Mike, Cadman. I know what you do for a living; I used to do almost the same thing when you were my boss. That is a hell of a lot more dangerous than getting up there on Sally."

Cadman eyed the horse named Sally, not convinced.

"Come on, up you go," Colten pointed to the stirrup. "You know how it's done."

Firming his lips, putting his boot into the stirrup, he gripped, "I cannot believe I am doing this, again. I vowed I would not sit a horse this year, but where am I?" He lifted himself up, swung a leg over the saddle, and sat down, "Sitting on top of one."

Colten handed him the reins, chuckled. "This time, you can't blame me. This was your idea, remember?"

"Don't remind me." He adjusted the cowboy hat on his head and felt like an idiot. "If I get bucked off and die, make sure you put on my tombstone, 'Died for no other reason than for the love of a woman'."

Grinning, Colten said, "You've got my word on it. Those damn females have a way of sneaking into a man's heart even when we're being careful." He stepped back. "Off you go. It's almost six-thirty, and Sara has been holding dinner back until this is over, and I'm hungry enough to eat a…,"

"Don't you dare say it."

"Horse." Colten's smile was as wide as the prairie.

"Dip shit."

"Do you remember how to get Sally going, or do you want me to slap her flanks?"

"Keep your hands to yourself. I can do it myself, and I'll get there at my own pace."

Colten raised his left hand, glanced at his watch. "I was hoping to eat before midnight."

"Har, har."

Cadman used the heels of his boots to gently prod the horse into the act of moving forward.

"That's painful to watch," Hunter said, coming to stand alongside his father. "I can walk faster than that."

Colten reached up, messed up his son's hair. "One day you might understand what loving a woman does to a man."

Hunter rolled his eyes, shook his head. "I am way too smart for that to happen," he said and began walking away.

Colten watched his second-oldest son strolling toward the house and thought, when I was your age, I felt the same way.

Inside the Fisher's home, Jacqueline was eyeing their housekeeper as though the woman had lost her mind. "Sara, I do not understand why supper is not being served. We always eat at six o'clock."

Sara wiped at the countertop with a dishcloth. "I told you, your husband asked me to hold off until he came into the house. He did not explain why."

Jacqueline could not wait to hear Colten's explanation, and for his sake, the explanation had better be a good one. She had some children looking at her as though they were about to starve. Especially Clinton. He might be twenty-one, but sometimes his autism, classified now as Pervasive Developmental Disorder Not Otherwise Specified, came out if they withheld food from him. He had learned how to curve his obsession over a delay in food, but she could see he was having a hard time coping if his slow rocking at the dining table was any indication.

"I think you can at least fix a plate for Clinton, or you can deal with the tantrum," she told the housekeeper.

Sara glanced into the dining room, picked up a plate immediately, and filled it with some of the boy's favorites. There was a time to listen to what your employer told you to do, and then there was a time to be practical.

Sara set the plate down in front of Clinton, and he pounced on it, reminding Kasey of Dolly. She had been here long enough to understand Clinton. Although he was an expert with horses and could interact with people very well, he had a few quirks that needed special attention.

Rosalinda and Charles smiled as Clinton dug into the plate full of food with gusto. "He does like his food," Charles commented, but when his own stomach growled, he looked at his wife and told her, "I am about to go into the kitchen and steal something to eat."

"Me too, papa!" Mason agreed.

Those at the table were about to do just that when from outside of the house, and through the open windows, Cadman's voice boomed, "Kasey Evans, I've come a' callin', and you best come out here."

Everyone looked at Kasey. Her eyes had grown wide as she stared toward the front of the house.

Donna said, "Is it my imagination, or is Uncle Cadman talking with some corny western accent?"

"You hear me, darlin'?" Cadman's voice boomed again.

Kasey could not believe her ears. He had been gone all night, and most of the day, and now he was making a demand?

She would see about that. She got up from the table and marched for the front door. Swinging it open, she stepped onto the porch and stopped dead in her tracks when her eyes landed on Cadman.

He was dressed head-to-toe in white, all the way from the cowboy hat on top of his head to the boots covering his feet. He was sitting on one of the ranch's quarter horses and staring at her as though daring her to laugh.

Laughter was the last thing on her mind as she stared at him, and her heart skipped a beat.

"Kasey Evans, I have come here to propose. I would like to get hitched if you'll have me." He managed to dismount without falling on his ass and walked up the steps and toward her until he was two feet away.

"Last night I drove all the way to Bismarck, and that is almost two hours from here." Cadman told her. "I had to spend the night in a hotel because nothing was open. Then I spent the whole damn day looking for this getup, and looking for this," He reached into his pocket, pulled out a small box. He got down on one knee and opened the lid of the box to reveal a ring set with an intense pink sapphire bordered by a graduated set of brilliant-cut diamonds.

Tears formed in her eyes. She was so touched by his romantic proposal; her throat was closed with emotion.

He stood up, closed the distance between them, took the ring out of the box, reached for her hand. "Will you marry me, Kasey Evans?" Before she could answer, he told her, "And I have the receipt for the ring. It's in my back pocket if you wanted to see the proof of purchase."

On a choked laugh, she threw herself into his arms. "Yes!" she exclaimed, kissing him on his mouth, his cheek, his chin, and back to his mouth. "Yes, I'll marry you, you wonderful, crazy man!"

Chapter Twenty-nine

Three days after the Fourth of July celebration at the F&L, Kasey and Cadman arrived back in Washington D.C., driving straight to Cadman's mother's house. It would be their first stop before going to Kasey's parents' home to pick up Dolly and then going home.

Pulling up in front of his mother's house, which was painted pink and had at least twenty plastic flamingos displayed throughout the yard, Cadman turned off the engine of his Firebird then sat in the driver's seat, unmoving.

Here he was, doing something he vowed would never happen, and he could not believe how nervous he was.

"Were we going in?" Kasey asked, looking at him, looking at the house.

"I'm thinking about it," he said.

"I thought the whole point of coming here was so you could introduce me to your mother."

Mutt barked from the back seat.

"And apparently Mutt wants to see his grandma," Kasey added.

"Maybe we should wait?" Cadman told her.

She giggled. "Cadman, honey, are you nervous?"

He narrowed his eyes at her. "Of course not." Whopper of a lie. He was already envisioning how this whole thing with his mother was going to go. Oh, I knew it!, his mother would say in that sing-song voice of hers. I knew you were lonely. "You don't know the woman, Kasey," he told her.

"And if we do not get out of the car and knock on her door, it will remain that way. Come on! I want to meet the woman."

"Mom's a little eccentric."

Kasey threw her head back and laughed. "I guessed that a long time ago, and I think those yard decorations are to die for. Maybe I should get some for our yard after we decide where we are going to live?"

He glowered at her. "No. No way in hell."

Her body shook with her laughter. "We can talk yard decorations later." She opened her door. "Come on. It's time to be a brave little soldier."

"Don't blame me for not warning you if she says something weird." Cadman climbed out from the vehicle, let Mutt out, and closed the door.

When he came around the car and helped her out, she hooked her arm through his as they took the first step toward the house. "It won't be that bad," she said, hoping it would be true. She had her own apprehensions over meeting his mother, but sitting in that car, wondering about the unknown, would resolve nothing.

Mutt ran up the sidewalk to the front door as though he knew there would be a treat waiting for him.

"Awh," Kasey said. "Isn't that sweet? He can't wait to see grandma."

"Because he knows the woman gives him at least six milk-bones when we visit. I'm lucky he doesn't puke in my car on the way home."

Kasey shook her head, laughed.

They reached the front door, and Cadman rang the doorbell.

"Hold your bloomers on!" A voice from inside shouted. "I'm coming!"

Mutt barked twice.

"Is that my grand dog?" they heard her say.

"Yes, mom!" Cadman shouted through the door.

The door swung open, and there stood his mother dressed in purple shorts and a pink sweater.

"Hi, mom," he said.

"Oh, my goodness. If it isn't my youngest. Visiting me before the end of the month."

He would not let her cause him guilt.

Mutt barked again.

His mother's attention went to the dog. "Don't you worry. I have a treat for you. Come on in, you silly old dog."

"Mom," Cadman said, "I want you to meet-"

"I do eat!" his mom told him.

Kasey almost laughed. Apparently, the woman needed a hearing aid.

Cadman shook his head. "No, mom. I want you to meet Kasey." He reached out his arm and pulled Kasey to his side to bring her to his mom's attention.

His mother's eyes traveled to the girl, scrutinizing. "Hello?" There was a question in her tone.

Kasey held up her left hand, showed his mother the ring. "I am going to marry your son," she told her future mother-in-law.

The older woman's eyes looked at the ring, and slowly, as understanding dawned, she allowed her eyes to travel back to Cadman. She said, "It's about time!" And tears leaped to her eyes. "Come in, come in!" she opened the door wider, stepped to the side for the couple to enter.

As they followed her into the living room, Cadman heard his mother say, "I knew you were lonely!"

Cadman rolled his eyes, and Kasey laughed.

"We can't stay long, mom. We need to stop at Kasey's parent's house and pick up her dog before going home."

Kasey swatted his arm. "He means cat, Mrs. Benson."

His mother sat down on the recliner. "I love cats! Now sit down and tell me how you got this boy of mine to ask you to marry him when no one else could get his attention."

"It's a long story," Kasey told her.

"You take as long as you need, young lady."

And Kasey told her about how she had accused him of shoplifting, then discovering they were neighbors.

His mother cackled. Like a witch. Cadman had never heard her do that before. "Are you all right, mom?"

Wiping tears of mirth from her eyes, she said, "Honey, I did the same thing to your dad, God rest his soul."

Cadman stared. "Excuse me?"

"I was seventeen. I was working at the Woolworth store when that handsome fella came in. When he came to where I was standing behind the counter to pay for the things he wanted to purchase, I tried to charge him for the hat on his head. It looked brand new to me, and we carried the same one's." She sat back in the recliner with a smile on her face as the memory of it flashed through her mind.

"How come I never heard that story before?" Cadman wanted to know. Then he looked at Kasey as something dawned on him.

Oh. My. Hell. He was going to marry someone like dear old mom.

"I made your father promise never to tell that story!" mom said. "I was so embarrassed by what I had done."

Kasey reached out and took Cadman's hand in hers as she told his mother, "I really like the colors of your living room." And it was the truth. Who would have thought the colors she picked out would look so good on these walls? "Maybe I should paint our living room like this when we find a house to share?"

"Absolutely not!" Cadman growled.

Kasey grinned at him. "We'll talk about it later."

His mother stood up, motioned for Kasey to follow. "Come into the kitchen, dear. I want to show you what you can do with your leftovers from the week. My cream of mushroom soup casserole is one of Cadman's favorite meals."

Cadman hung his head, put his face in his hands. Now would be a good time for someone to shoot him. Perhaps he had been too hasty in giving Ford his resignation from the fieldwork.

They visited with his mother for over an hour before telling her goodbye, then drove to Kasey's parents to pick up Dolly and make introductions to her parents.

Mutt eyed Dolly with suspicion and gave a testing growl. When Dolly hissed, Mutt backed up with his ears laid back.

"Oh dear," Kasey said. "I hope this isn't going to be a problem."

Cadman leaned down, gave her a kiss. "They'll argue a bit, but I think they will work it out, eventually. We did."

Looking up at the man she loved, Kasey said, "We certainly did."

Cadman told her, "I guess all I ever needed was someone like you to turn my world upside down."

"I promise to keep you on your toes," she told him.

He chuckled. "I'm sure you will at that."

When they arrived home, it was to see a car parked in Kasey's driveway, and someone standing at her door.

"Hey, Sandy," Kasey called out as she climbed from Cadman's car carrying Dolly. "What brings you by? I'm just getting home from a wonderful vacation to the Badlands of North Dakota. You should go there one day."

"I might just do that," Sandy told her. "Would you like me to hold Dolly for you so you can unlock your door?"

"That would be great, thanks." But before Kasey could hand the cat to her friend, Cadman stepped onto the porch.

"Hey, Doc Hoover, what's up?"

Kasey looked between the two. "This is my friend Sandy Rinehart. Her last name is not Hoover."

Sandy chuckled as Cadman stared. "He knows my name, Kasey. But he's too ornery to use it."

"You two know each other?" Kasey exclaimed.

"Doc Hoover is the psychiatrist for Task Force Ghost," Cadman explained.

Smiling, Sandy said to Cadman, "Well, that must mean the two of you have gotten serious enough for you to tell her that."

"Hold it," Kasey said. "Back up one minute. Sandy, you knew who my neighbor was when I had lunch with you?"

The doctor nodded.

"That explains so much," Kasey said.

"I'm glad you're not having brain fog, dear," Cadman told her. "But I am as confused as hell."

"She's the one who encouraged me to have you over to my place for dinner that first time, even though I thought you were a drug-using psychopath!"

Cadman stared.

Sandy shrugged. "Hey, you moved next door to him. I just happened to know the two of you were right for each other. You can thank me by inviting me to the wedding. Now, let me see the ring!"

“Drug using—What?!” Cadman roared, his mind taking a moment to process what Kasey had told the doc.

“I saw you in an ally once with a homeless man. I thought you were buying drugs. I was considering trying to council you that night at dinner, but after you told me you worked for the Secret Service, I assumed you were on a case.”

“You have a bad habit of assuming things where I’m concerned,” he griped.

Kasey handed Dolly to Sandy, wrapped her arms around him. “I promise not to do that anymore.”

“Ha. I’m sure I’ll do something to cause your suspicions to rise up.”

“Well, maybe,” she laughed and kissed him.

Someone Like You

Epilogue

One year later

Cadman and Kasey were married the following summer, at the F&L Ranch south of Medora, two days before the fourth of July. By having the wedding at the ranch, Colten and Jacqueline could attend, and Kasey wanted Cadman's best friend and his wife to be part of the ceremony.

The wedding had been a small affair, with only a select few invited.

Kasey's parents were there, and of course, the Fisher clan. The Lafayette's arrived from Paris two days before the ceremony.

Cadman's mother, brother, and his family were also there. His mother cried the entire time, happy that her son found someone like Kasey.

President Carter, who had won the election the previous year, gifted the couple with a bag of peanuts. And the promise to give Cadman a month's leave before Carter expected him to report back to work. Cadman was no longer required to be in the field with his team but would run the operations of Task Force Ghost from behind a desk.

A few of Cadman's team members were invited to the wedding, which, Kasey thought in hindsight, might not have been the best idea. They kidnapped her after the ceremony and did not return her to the angry groom until one hour after the first dance of the night was to begin.

Kasey thoroughly enjoyed her outing with the team, who escorted her to the town of Dickinson, thirty-six miles east of Medora. They bar-hopped, taking her to six or more different places. Cadman, stuck behind at the ranch, spent the entire time pacing and making vows to ship the men off to Siberia forever.

For those at the wedding, who did not know Cadman had the power to do what he claimed, he sounded like a crazy man.

As the months passed, Kasey and Cadman sold both of their homes and purchased one that was double the size of the old ones. Surprisingly, Mutt and Dolly adjusted to one another without too much fuss. Once the animals established boundaries with the other, the disagreements were far and few between.

The Benson's developed a comfortable routine. Cadman's job was now nine-to-five Monday through Friday most of the time. Kasey's job as a manager did not give her a set schedule. However, they arranged date nights whenever they could, so there would always be quality time together.

As the years passed, they continued to make the yearly trip to Medora, North Dakota, to celebrate the fourth of July with the Fisher's and Lafayette's. Neither of them regretted not having children of their own but dearly loved watching Cadman's nieces and nephews, and the Fisher clan and Lafayette's children slowly maturing into young adults.

Cadman's only regret as the years passed was his inability to locate and arrest Pierre Bellefeuille, but that did not mean he gave up trying. Whenever there was the slightest lead to a possible location of the man, Cadman would travel to wherever the potential sighting occurred, always hoping this time the information was reliable and he could put Pierre once again behind bars, or a bullet through his head.

A few years later and believing he was destined for a life of adventure and purpose, Hunter announced on his fifteenth birthday that he planned to join the Navy as soon as he turned seventeen, with his parents' permission, of course.

His parents listened to his declaration with a mixture of pride and trepidation. They had always encouraged their son's passion for service and adventure, but the thought of him entering such a dangerous and unpredictable profession filled them with worry.

And yet, they couldn't deny the fire in Hunter's eyes, the determination in his voice. He had always been a natural leader, quick to take charge and make hard decisions. They knew he would excel in the Navy or whatever occupation he chose.

Cadman could not deny he'd eagerly waited, and hoped, for the day Hunter chose military life. He had seen Hunter's potential from the first martial arts tournament he'd won. And with his eidetic memory, he would be a valuable asset to his team.

About the author.

Thank you for purchasing this book. I hope you enjoyed it. The Fisher/Lafayette Saga continues with Spitfire. Continue reading for a sneak peek.

I have lived in Bismarck, North Dakota, all my life. Medora, North Dakota, holds a special place in my heart.

This work, Someone Like You, is the third book in the Fisher/Lafayette series. Do not forget to pick up your copy of Colten and Jacqueline's story: If There Hadn't Been You, and Charles and Rosalinda's story, Now and Forever.

Keep reading for a sneak peek of Spitfire!

You can find me:

Web site:www.jrzimmer.com

Email: jrzimmer17@yahoo.com

Spitfire

by J.R. Zimmer

Prelude

May 1981

Was he going to kill her?

Amanda Anderson quivered with fear and apprehension as his ice-blue eyes continued their intense stare. Once she had thought his eyes breathtaking; now they were angry and hateful.

And definitely full of rage.

She supposed she could not blame him for what he was so obviously feeling as he stood there, glaring. And she admitted she had brought this hatred upon herself. But she would not apologize for what she'd done.

Hadn't she warned him? It was a pity he had not taken her seriously when she told him what she could make happen if he kept refusing to give her what she wanted from him.

Still wanted from him, but now that he experienced her wrath, she doubted he was any more willing to comply with her wishes.

"Why?" he hissed, causing Amanda to jerk with surprise. He had been standing there, in the middle of her living room, for well over two minutes, not saying anything. Only holding her captive with those fury filled eyes.

She hadn't anticipated he might somehow escape from prison.

Her eyes left his for a moment, taking in the change in his appearance. He had been thinner when he first came to work at the ranch, a little over a year ago. Now he was more muscular in all the right places. His dark brown hair, once cropped short, hung to his shoulders, kept back by a blue bandana tied around his forehead.

The past six months had enhanced his handsomeness and sexual allure. The only noticeable fault that had not been there before he went to

prison was the fading red scare just under his chin. As though someone had thought to slice his throat but missed.

He was positively yummy to look at, even in his rage. Regardless of thinking her life might be in danger, Amanda's body tingled with sexual tension.

She forced herself to relax. Perhaps he had learned his lesson and was here to, finally, comply with her desire, though she would obviously have to calm him down.

In a purr, she said, "Now, Jake, darling…."

"Why!?" his outburst caused her to jerk back.

He advanced, grabbed her shoulders, and shook her until her teeth rattled. "God damn it, why?!"

For one moment, her lust was forgotten as she wondered, once again, if he were here to kill her and she could do nothing if that was his intent.

Nor was there anyone here to prevent Jake from following through with his intent, whatever it might be. She was alone at the ranch tonight. Her husband left a few hours ago, traveling to New York on some business trip she could not care less about. The few hired hands were gone for the evening, doing whatever they did for entertainment, and the housekeeper had the night off.

For one fleeting second, she wondered how long it would be before anyone found her body.

Suddenly he released her. She fell back. The air rushed from her lungs as she landed hard on the couch.

He loomed over her. The thought the image brought to mind had her thinking, hoping, he was actually going to take advantage of her.

She positively hoped that was what he was here to do. She would have hated having died without knowing what it was like to have him between her legs as he pounded into her.

She had spent the first three months of his employment to this ranch desperately trying to seduce him, without results and much to the chagrin of her vanity. She was a woman who could have any man she chose at the snap of her fingers.

But not him. Oh no, he was the one man to have turned her down time and time again. It enraged her and motivated her to fabricate the lie that had gotten him locked up.

She found witnesses to confirm her accusations. All male, of course. What she had had to do for each of them, for their claims to have observed the alleged theft of her husband's prized Appaloosa stallion, had been immensely satisfying for each of them.

She was, admittedly, a slut.

Breathlessly she asked, "Are you going to rape me?"

His face contorted as though a foul odor suddenly entered the room. "I don't fuck old ladies," he snapped.

Her face flamed hot. "How dare you!"

"How dare I!?" his explosion vibrated throughout the entire twenty-seven room mansion. "You accused me of stealin' Thomas's purebred stallion! You got me thrown into prison! And all because I wouldn't screw you, and you have the fuckin' gall to be angry with me?!"

Amanda pushed herself up from the couch and stood before him as though ready to battle. "What did you come here for, Jake?" she shouted back, placing her fists on her slim hips. Evidently, she was wrong on both of her assumptions.

He was not here to kill her, and he was not going to take his pants off.

"I want to know why you made up that lie about me! I was never anywhere near Thomas' appaloosa that night, and you know it!"

"Of course, I do! But I warned you that last time you refused to take me to bed. I get what I want, or there are consequences."

"So, you sent the law after me?!" Hearing her admit the truth almost rendered him speechless.

How was it that throughout his entire life, he kept winding up running into spiteful women who only wanted one thing from him?

But this one was absolutely the worst of them all.

When he came to this ranch to work cattle, and everything else required concerning the operation of the place, this woman threw herself at him at every turn. He did not deny the fact she was pretty for a woman

her age. He suspected she might be around fifty or fifty-five, but she did not appeal to him.

Never had.

But out of all those women he'd encountered over the years, this one had been vindictive enough to accomplish having him thrown in jail because he said no to her invitations to bed her.

Not that the jury sitting in that kangaroo court heard that reason. They convicted him of stealing a horse he hadn't, anyway.

It was too unbelievable.

He should have hightailed it out of there the first time she came on to him. But he had not expected she was malicious enough to manipulate a tale that would convince the judge to send him to prison.

Amanda, he discovered, had every man in the area at her beck and call.

Perhaps if he had swallowed his pride and contacted his father, the trumped-up charges would have been stopped instantly. But he had not believed anyone would believe that ridiculous accusation of hers. By the time he realized they really were going to lock him up, it had been too late.

Would he have called his old man had he known what the outcome of that joke of a trial was going to be? Hard to say, although he hated his parents enough to consider the answer would have been, no.

Amanda shrugged.

She moved away from him, her slim figure settling gracefully into the plush recliner next to the couch. Once comfortable, she studied him openly. He was the most handsome man she had ever encountered, and young, about twenty-five or twenty-six, if her memory served. His muscled arms, showcased by the torn-off sleeves of his dull gray T-shirt, instantly revived her fantasy of having him in her bed.

She sighed inwardly. How dare Jake Harper refuse her?

"Why, Amanda?" his voice was not as loud as before, but the fury was still there. "Just because I wouldn't...."

"Exactly!" she screeched. "I have never been refused!"

He stared at her. This whole situation would be laughable if it had not honestly happened. No one in their right mind would believe his story if he told it, and he was not about to tell anyone this ludicrous tale.

It took six months, after the new sheriff was appointed to replace the corrupt one and before the election could be held, to even begin investigating Jake's case. The new sheriff would have started sooner, but the previous sheriff, who had been a pawn of Amanda's, had deliberately left the office in complete disarray, making any immediate investigation nearly impossible.

Jake would always be grateful the new officer was law-abiding enough to investigate his case. The work revealed the central lie: Jake was in prison for stealing a horse that was still grazing on the Anderson ranch. Had Jake actually taken the appaloosa, the animal would undoubtedly be missing.

Maybe he should have stayed in Texas. He had gone from one boiling pot into another, and he would like to know how he'd managed that.

Well, this bad dream was about to take care of itself. As long as Jake played his part and did not give in to the urge to strangle Amanda, she would take his place in a prison cell.

Jake had never been a man who would hit a woman. Nor had he ever desired to kill one, but he wanted to kill this one. He itched to wrap his hands around her neck and squeeze the life out of her.

But he was not going back to jail. He would avoid that like the plague. But it would satisfy him to know Amanda would no longer be free to cause some other unsuspecting guy hardship. And it elated him, knowing he would have a clean slate once this drama played out.

Man, oh man, had he definitely learned that hell hath no fury as a woman scorned.

"I have a hard time understandin' why," Jake told her, "the wife of a prominent rancher, would sink so low as to destroy someone else's life just because their advances were turned down."

Amanda reminded him so much of his mother it made him sick.

The mention of her aging husband brought contempt to her voice. She married Thomas Anderson five years ago only because he was rich, and she liked beautiful things.

"I detest my husband!" she shouted, the veins in her neck standing out. "He is an old man and hasn't a clue how to make love to a woman. He should have died years ago! He is eighty-five years old, for Christ's sake. But no, the old buzzard keeps ongoing. I'm hoping one of the men around here will want me enough to get rid of him for me since Tomas doesn't seem capable of dropping dead on his own!"

Footsteps echoed from within the outer hallway.

Amanda froze. Her eyes were wide as she turned toward the sound. Jake's face remained impassive when he saw the two people entering the room. He knew they were in the house, staying out of Amanda's sight until the right moment to reveal themselves came along.

Amanda's eyes bulged when she saw not only her husband but the new sheriff with him.

She had tried to get that new lawman into her bed. Not because she found him attractive, but men were easily enough controlled if given the right motivation. In Amanda's experience, the right motivation had always been sex.

Obviously, she was losing her touch.

It took the conniving woman three seconds to recover from her shock. She hoped Thomas's hearing was worse than his lovemaking.

She leaped from the chair and rushed to the elderly man's side. "Darling!" she cried, "Oh, thank heavens you're here! He came here to kill me!" She threw her arms around Thomas as though her life depended upon it.

"Kill you, dear wife?" Thomas Anderson questioned tonelessly, feeling every bit as old and weary as his years suggested he should be. It was hard to admit to making mistakes and having married Amanda had been the biggest mistake of his life.

No. He knew that was not true. His biggest mistake had been allowing Amanda to convince him Jake Harper had stolen from him when the kid was a hard worker and an honest man. However, Thomas's eyes were

wide open now, and he saw the gold-digger for what she was: a calculating bitch. But he was not the one who had suffered Amanda's vindictiveness. Jake Harper had been on the receiving end, and Thomas wondered how one made amends to someone who had been allowed to lose six months of their life because of his weakness? If Harper never forgave him, he would understand.

Thomas answered his soon to be ex-wife by saying, "I don't believe he will kill you, but if the Sheriff weren't here, I would be pleased to do so myself."

Sheriff Watts sighed, "Sorry, Thomas. I wish these were the old days, and I could just turn my back. I wouldn't blame you a bit if you wrung her scrawny neck."

Amanda noticeably stiffened. "Thomas, what is this all about?" She pushed tears past her lashes as she tried to look innocent in the performance she was about to give. If someone were to give out awards in the real world for falsifying emotion, Amanda would have owned several of them by now.

She reached out, tentatively running her hand down the sleeve of his arm, confused when her touch did not take away the hate she saw for her in his eyes. The old buzzard should be assuring her he had not meant to imply he wanted her dead. Never mind the fact she daily hoped he would keel over; this ranch would then be hers, and she would gladly sell it off to the first bidder. But Thomas was not embracing her. Was, in fact, looking at her with so much hate and anger, she had a terrifying moment to consider that she was about to lose everything she had worked so hard for.

"Thomas!" she exclaimed in fear, and it wasn't an act now.

Thomas pushed his wife away from him and shoved her toward the sheriff. "Get her out of my house."

Sheriff Watts wasted no time handcuffing the fifty-five-year-old aging beauty.

"Thomas!" Amanda screamed as she tried to resist arrest. How dare they do this to her!

She cursed her husband, the Sheriff, Jake, and God almighty to hell and back as the sheriff forcefully pulled her from the room.

Jake watched as the Sheriff and Amanda disappeared from sight and marveled as the woman continued to insist she had done nothing wrong. Evidently, the woman believed she had been the victim this night.

Jake hoped Amanda would rot in jail for a good long time. But he was honest enough with himself to know she would probably seduce every guard in the place to make her stay behind bars enjoyable, and not a punishment.

Thomas Anderson stepped forward, extending an overstuffed envelope toward Jake. "I can only say I'm sorry, kid," Thomas said, sighing and shaking his head. "I should have known all those months ago you were innocent. I've suspected Amanda of infidelity for years, but I kept turning my back on the truth, desperate to believe she loved me. But what she did to you..." Thomas trailed off, unable to finish the thought. There were no words sufficient to give the younger man. Nothing he could say would return the months robbed from Jake because Thomas had been such a fool.

Debating whether to accept Thomas's offering, Jake eyed the envelope which, he knew, was a blatant payment for a guilty conscience.

After a moment he took the packet, justifying it as back pay for the six months of life he'd lost. The money was meaningless to him; he planned to donate it to charity. He didn't utter a word to the man who held the power to have shut down that entire mockery of a trial before it began.

As Jake turned away, Tomas said, "There's enough cash in there," Thomas indicated the envelope he held in his hand, "to get you started wherever you wind up." He sighed, adding, "There's also a letter of recommendation- " Thomas looked at him, moisture in his eyes. "I don't know what else to say. Thanks for your help lacks in its intent. You've paid a high price for my turning my back on Amanda's selfish ways." He offered his hand for a parting shake but did not take offense when the younger man did not accept it.

Jake clutched the envelope in his fist as he made his way to the front door. He was so completely finished with the whole ordeal that he didn't

even spare the old man the courtesy of telling him to go to fuck off. Walking straight through the door, Jake headed directly to the brand-new, jacked-up Ford pickup truck. The truck was yet another payoff from Thomas Anderson, a replacement for Jake's vehicle, which the man had sold while Jake was in prison.

That had probably pissed him off more than anything else. He had loved that truck. It had been custom painted with wild horses on either side.

This truck was plain ol' black.

Yuck.

Well, he supposed he could get this one painted but did not know if he wanted to bother. Custom paint jobs took time, and Jake was not planning to stay around here longer than necessary.

Jake tossed the envelope into the glove compartment without looking at its contents. He knew the sizable amount of hundred-dollar bills it contained.

Gazing out the windshield of the truck, he almost laughed as he thought of that money. If Anderson knew how much Jake was worth, he probably would not have been as generous with his guilty conscious payoff.

Looking at the road leading from this ranch, Jake had no idea where he wanted to go next.

He did know he would not go back home to Texas.

Turning the ignition key, Jake sat back in the seat and almost broke out in hysterical laughter. It struck him funny, in a cynical way, that when he had left Texas to be rid of his mother, he had found her clone in a little nothing of a town north of Casper, Wyoming.

Chapter One

The child stood in the doorway of his parent's room watching as his mother, sitting in front of the vanity mirror, applied cosmetics to her already impossibly beautiful face. The child, although only five years old, knew his mother was lovely.

He could not remember a time when he had not known this fact. And, if for some unforeseen reason he would think differently, there were countless people in this Texas community to remind him. Every time he was with his mother in town, people they passed would whisper among themselves, "Oh, there goes Clair Harper. I declare she is the most beautiful creature in this state."

Men would whistle in a way that disturbed the child but caused the recipient to smile coyly over her shoulder at them and wink in such a way the boy would frown. It did not seem right that his mother would look at other men like that when she never appeared to give the same affection on her husband.

His father was not at home. Gone for the weekend, attending a horse sale in Dallas. Gregory Harper's one true passion seemed to be horses. The man had built an Appaloosa horse empire from the ground up, and today that ranch was world-famous for the trophy-winning mounts produced each year.

Young Jake had gained his love of horses from his father. Above anything, he would rather be with his father in the corrals, working the horses, then sitting with his nanny reading books. Or learning some silly nonsense Clair thought he should be educated on. Such as the violin,

which was her latest idea to add culture to her only child. Jake shuddered with the thought. He hated the squawking instrument more than the piano she gifted him last year for his fourth birthday.

Clair wanted, for reasons known only to herself, her son to be musically inclined when there was not any talent. Jake grew to hate the sight of the grand piano with each passing lesson.

The grand piano now sat in the ballroom, alone and forgotten. Thank God the instructor had finally dared to inform Clair her son did not have any talent for the ivory keyed instrument.

The woman's honesty had gotten her fired. But Jake felt liberated when the woman's bags were packed, and she was gone. He was free to enjoy his toy trucks in the sandbox in the backyard whenever he wasn't working horses with his father. He may have just turned five, but it was clear to anyone who cared to notice that the child had been born for the saddle. That was his natural talent, and one his mother refused to acknowledge. It was her belief that anything resembling Gregory Harper had to be crushed. One month later, she handed Jake the violin, insisted he learn it, and refused his pleads to ride the ranch with his father.

Jake had vowed to find some way to break that new instrument of torture and had not cared one whit that Clair would become enraged by the act of rebellion. Fortunately, it had not come to that. His father, during a rare moment of backbone, had taken a stand against his wife and told Clair to stop trying to make his son into a sissy.

For the time being, Jake was free from cursed musical instruction. If Clair knew just how much her son relished that fact, she would have instantly found some other device to push into his hands. But Jake was smart enough to keep his joy to himself. It was that or have Clair in an angry rage.

The boy realized his mother was no longer focused on her self-pampering when she caught his image in the mirror's reflection. Their gazes locked: hers filled with disapproval, his with sadness and loneliness.

If only she would love him. Just a little. Better still if he would not desire her attention. But he was only a child, and she was his mother. He longed for the affection she held back from him.

Clair sighed and turned eloquently towards him. The carefully waxed brows that normally arched gracefully over her almond-shaped blue eyes lowered in an unattractive manner as she regarded him for several moments before speaking. "Why are you not in bed?"

The tone he knew well enough. It told him his mother wished he were anywhere but where she was.

He had interrupted her, and she was not happy about it.

"I," he hesitated. "I cannot sleep. Would you read me a story?"

Her laugh was dismissive. "Go find Alice. You have a nanny. She will be more than happy to read to you." Clair turned back to the mirror, picked up one of her cosmetic brushes, and began stroking her face with it, dismissing him with, "It is what she gets paid for, for heaven's sake."

Although he was aware she would respond in such a manner, it didn't stop him from asking. He had predicted her reaction, and it only fueled his rebellious spirit. "Papa would read to me!" he declared bravely, standing tall with his head held high, challenging her to refute his statement.

"Well," Clair sneered, "he is not here now, is he?"

The boy hung his head, refusing to give in to the urge to cry. Clair would like it if she knew she had struck his heart, but he learned early enough not to show her the power she had to hurt him.

He swallowed a few times, trying to find a voice that would not betray him when a loud buzzing sound seemed to come from somewhere distant. It was faint at first, then louder as the room before him faded to mist, and his eyes snapped open to the here and now.

Jake ripped the alarm clock from the nightstand and threw it against the wall.

He fell back heavily onto the bed as his foggy brain reminded him, he was no longer a little boy. He was a grown man, in a hotel room, and the alarm clock he had just broken did not belong to him.

"Fuck," he groaned as he reached for the spare pillow and covered his face with it. He hated those memories, those intrusive dreams. He needed no reminders as to why he was not in Texas anymore.

As far as he was concerned, his parents were dead to him.

At least the dream had not been one of Clair after he turned seventeen. That's when she began giving him the attention no son wanted from their mother.

It made his skin crawl.

He viciously shook his head, wanting to shake the past away.

Sitting up, he reached for the television controller. Flipping the TV on, he placed his feet on the floor and headed for the bathroom. He might as well shower and checkout. The sooner he was out of Wyoming, the better. He would have made it across the border last night if it had not been so late in the evening when all that business with Amanda took place. But once he hit the highway, and the miles rolled away, he felt the tension in him wearing him down. By the time he reached Gillette, he decided to spend the night here before moving on to he did not know where.

After the shower, he wiped the fogged-up mirror with a single swipe of the towel he used to dry off with.

He finished shaving and regarded his reflection. While women swooned over his looks, he cursed them. The mirror showed his blue eyes, but it failed to reflect the deep-seated anger and hardness that had hardened him over the years. He wondered what he had done to deserve a life marked with nothing but ill fate when it came to women.

He sighed heavily and pushed the question down. He needed time to regroup from the last few months, and he wanted to be someplace where there wasn't some damn deceitful female hanging around.

For a moment, he considered cutting his hair back to a more conservative style but knowing it would piss Clair off had him forgetting the notion. There was nothing more enjoyable than going against mommy dearest to give him a fresh start to the day.

He dressed in a pair of faded jeans and a short-sleeved T-shirt and tied a blue bandana around his forehead to keep the hair from his eyes. After that, he packed up the meager items he bothered to bring inside with him last night and headed out of the room to the main lobby.

He ignored the flirtatious blonde behind the counter as much as he could during the checkout process. She was not holding her interest in him at bay, but he was not in the mood for anything other than breakfast.

When he asked her where he could get a decent stack of pancakes, her answering frown told him she was not used to being ignored in such a manner.

Too bad for her, he thought as he picked up his duffle bag from where he had dropped it on the lobby floor and headed out the door.

He did not give her another thought for the rest of his life.

He found the little café the girl directed him to without a hitch. Hell, if a person got lost in Gillette, Wyoming, they did not have the brains of an apple peel.

A waitress showed him to a corner booth. He placed his order immediately, without glancing at a menu, and then asked if there was a newspaper he could read while he waited.

"Sure, Sugar," the middle-aged woman drawled, snapped the gum she was chewing, and winked at him. "I can find yah one." And she did, in record time. "There you go, Sugar." She winked again. "Anything else I can do for you?"

Inwardly Jake shuddered. Couldn't women leave him alone?

"No," he answered, "thanks," and he snapped the paper open in a dismissive gesture. He felt, rather than saw, the woman's disappointed frown before she left him to move onto another table and leaving him blissfully alone.

He scanned the news and found nothing of interest.

He turned to the help-wanted section on a sudden whim. It wasn't that he needed employment, as he was, in fact, quite wealthy, having inherited a substantial trust fund from his grandparents when he was ten. However, having cut all ties to his parents, he preferred not to touch that account. His primary motivation was to maintain secrecy about his location and proving to his mother; correction, his parents, that he was perfectly capable of succeeding without relying on the Harper family fortune.

He knew, with absolute certainty, that if he touched his account, the bank manager, Mr. Todd, would run straight to Clair and reveal where the money had been sent. Jake was determined to prevent that from happening. Maintaining his secrecy was also why he contacted absolutely no one at the ranch following his arrest on the bogus charge. The thought of reaching out for help never once formed in his mind, not even after he was imprisoned.

As far as anyone knew, he was not related to the rich Texas Harpers, and he intended it to remain that way for possibly the rest of his life.

As he scanned the paper, his eyes fell on a notice that seemed to leap off the page at him. The lengthy size of the ad would draw eyes, but its contents spoke to Jake in such a way he could not resist rereading it:

Wanted: Full-time working Foreman.

F & L Ranch is a family-owned establishment located 20 miles South of Medora, ND.

We are seeking a single, mature, honest, hard-working man between the ages of 25-30, who would be a full-time assistant, Foreman. Expected to help maintain headquarters, string fences, organize guided tours, and oversee part-time summer employees. Must have excellent communication skills and enjoy being around children. Experienced horseman required, able to start young horses, maintain equipment, weld, trim, and shoe. Help with hunting tours during the winter season and anything else needed by the head of family. The F & L Ranch believes that ranching is more than just a job and is more than a career. It's a lifestyle. Excellent pay and benefits to include private efficiency apartment with own kitchen and bath.

Prefer application done in person, otherwise, send resume to F & L Ranch.

C/O Colten Fisher.

Jake leaned back, smiling. The job sounded made to order, and the fact it was in North Dakota- Well hell, Clair would not think to look for him there if she was looking at all when the woman still believed wild Indian's roamed the plans. Clair's opinion of the Dakota's had always been they were a godforsaken place. But right now, to Jake's way of thinking, it just might prove to be his saving grace.

He glanced up at the date on the paper, noting today's date. It was the middle of May. Hopefully, the job had not been filled yet.

If his geography was correct, which it had better be considering the sum of money Clair spent on private tutors for him, he was not that far from the South Dakota border.

He would check the map in his truck to be sure. If he was not mistaken, the location of this F&L Ranch wasn't much farther once he passed through the edge of South Dakota and crossed the border into North Dakota.

With a plan in mind, Jake folded the paper just as his breakfast order arrived. No, he did not need the job. The money Thomas Anderson handed him in that envelope last night would serve him for a while if he chose to spend it instead of donating it.

He shoved the half-eaten breakfast away. Time to hit the road. With any luck, once he reached North Dakota, the only women he would have to deal with would be little old ladies, far past their prime, who wanted nothing more than a horse guided tour into the Badlands.

Fisher/Lafayette Saga

If There Hadn't Been You
Now and Forever
Someone Like You
Spitfire
Something Magical
Coming Home (Free Ebook when signing up for my newsletter at www.jrzimmer.com. Not available anywhere else.
The Dreamer
Eagle's Wolf

www.ingramcontent.com/pod-product-compliance
Lightning Source LLC
LaVergne TN
LVHW050622100826
845148LV00011B/1691
* 9 7 8 1 7 3 7 6 2 6 9 0 9 *